Punch

J. R. Park

Other books by J. R. Park:

TERROR BYTE
UPON WAKING

Further books by the Sinister Horror Company:

BURNING HOUSE – Daniel Marc Chant
CLASS THREE – Duncan P. Bradshaw
MALDICION - Daniel Marc Chant

*Visit JRPark.co.uk and SinisterHorrorCompany.com for further
information on these and other coming titles.*

PUNCH

J. R. Park

SINISTER
HORROR
COMPANY

Punch
Second edition

First Published in 2014
This edition 2015

Cover artwork by Laura Coats
lacoats.webs.com
www.facebook.com/lacoatsart
www.etsy.com/uk/shop/LACoatsART

Back cover photography by Stuart Park
likebreathing.com

ISBN-13: 978-0-9932793-2-4

JRPark.co.uk

ACKNOWLEDGEMENTS

Thank you to Stuart Park and Daryl Mazelin for reading through my early drafts and providing me with the helpful and welcome feedback.

Thank you to Michelle Cook whose love of children's TV inspired the spark that started this tale and gave me a way in to horror fiction.

I'd also like to thank Hannah Filer for the enormous help in smoothing out the story whilst I was writing it as a film script a few years earlier.

For Hannah, because every time I write a book I hope
one day you'll read it.

1

J. R. Park

Neon signs selling candyfloss flickered their nauseating and tasteless glow against the darkening background of a building storm. Although it was mid afternoon the clouds had strangled the daylight from the sky and long shadows plunged boarded up, abandoned shops into a threatening darkness. Even those buildings that remained open for business looked like dying carcasses of beasts from a more successful age. The paintwork had blistered and peeled from their frames, exposed as they were to the harsh winters of this coastal town. Crude graffiti tattooed the promenade, a reminder to the lack of money and care with which the town had been looked after.

It had been a wet and windy winter and February showed no sign of getting any better. What little trade the summer holiday season had brought seemed like a distant memory to the inhabitants of Stanswick Sands as they tried to remain positive through these desperately grim times. They held on to hope that the outdated amusements and beautiful coastline could attract more visitors when the sun finally shone again.

Stanswick Sands. The Best in British Seaside.

The sign stood at the border of the town like the fossilised remains from a bygone era slowly dragged to extinction by cheap airlines, expensive fuel prices and economic recessions. It rattled and shook in the wind but the faded painting of the happy family on the beach with their 1950's grins continued to smile absurdly through the adversity.

A coach drove along a winding road passing the sign, its exterior was equally as grubby and unclean. It had set off on its travels in a far cleaner condition, but the four hour journey had seen it battle through some horrendous storms and water logged roads. It had not escaped the journey without some grimy mementos of its clashes with nature.

The coach had started full from the city but as it drew to its final destination the number of passengers dwindled to only a handful. Martin Powell had been on the coach for the full four hours and had been very nervous when he first climbed the stairs of the vehicle to take his seat. He looked ill at ease and out of place with the world around him. His brown suit looked dated and worn. It was at least two sizes too big and hung off his sleight, fifty year old frame like bed sheets draped over a chair. His hair was grey and thinning, it was neatly cut and styled although the comb-over did not hide the approaching baldness.

As the coach journey continued he had begun to relax and a smile began to appear on his face when they passed the sign. Stanswick Sands was fast turning from a memory to a welcome actuality.

As Martin's mood lightened he began to strike up a conversation with a woman named Grete and her seven year old son Kaspar. Despite the talking around him Kaspar had almost his full concentration focused on a handheld games console he was eagerly playing.

'Here we come now,' said Martin excitedly as they began to approach the promenade. He looked out the window of the coach with child-like eyes. 'It's such a lovely place. I couldn't think of anywhere else I would rather be. Look there's the beach and there's the pier,' he exclaimed, pointing them out as they came into view. 'Can you see it?'

Martin directed his question to Kaspar who looked up briefly, gave an unimpressed, 'Oh yeah', then went back to his computer game.

'Don't be so rude Kaspar!' his mother Grete spoke with an accent that Martin placed as somewhere from Eastern Europe or possibly Russia. He had not been the most traveled man in his fifty years.

'Kids today hey?' Martin joked. 'I can't believe it's been ten years since I saw the place. Oh look the Maze of Mirrors is still here. I can't believe it's still standing!'

He pointed to a single storey wooden building that seemed to shake slightly from the influence of the coastal wind. The entrance was painted in faded red and yellow stripes and framed in a row of red light bulbs that flashed in a random sequence, revealing a number of them to no longer be working. Above the doorway a sign proclaimed in letters that ended in tails like lightning bolts: *The World Famous Maze Of Mirrors.*

Ignoring Kaspar's indifference to his previous comment Martin turned to speak to the boy again, 'That used to be such a popular attraction with all the youngsters. Maybe you'll give it a go whilst you're here, it's much more fun than your computers.'

Kaspar did not even look up this time but screwed his face in mild irritation and continued with his game.

'I loved the Maze of Mirrors,' Martin continued, 'I could practically do the thing blind folded.' Sensing he had lost his young audience Martin turned to Grete. 'You are going to have such a lovely time here on holiday, but if you need a guide, someone to show you and little Kaspar around I'd be happy to oblige.'

'Thanks, that would be great,' Grete replied with a sincere smile.

'That's my address,' Martin jotted his address down on a piece of paper and handed it to her. 'Call round anytime. If not, I'm sure we'll bump into each other. It isn't a very big town. And even lovelier for it.'

The coach pulled in on the high street and its doors opened.

'This is my stop,' Martin said as he stood up placing a brown trilby on his head, 'yours will be the next one. Good day Grete. Good day little Kaspar.'

Like an old fashioned gent he tipped his hat to them as he gave his farewells and stepped off the coach.

He could immediately taste the salty air on his lips as the wind blew against his face. Looking around in wonder he stared past the view of urban decay, finding deeper beauty in the long sought familiarity that these simple sights brought him. His smile grew to a beam as he took a large, lungful of sea air through his nostrils, relishing in every sensation his surroundings presented. At first he didn't even mind the rain, but the storm became too great to ignore. Martin hunched his shoulders protecting his neck from the drips that ran down his hat and made his way into a small café facing the sea front.

The Minstrel café was brightly lit and it took a moment for Martin's eyes to adjust. When they did he saw a well-kept and clean establishment. It was sparsely populated with elderly customers washing delicately crafted cakes down with cups of tea. They quietly gossiped amongst themselves and took no notice of Martin as he made his way to the counter.

Behind the counter stood a nineteen year old girl, her brown, curly hair ended in ringlets as it rested softly on the shoulders of her pink, diner uniform. Her mouth masticated very deliberately on some chewing gum as she looked out the window onto the view of the sea crashing against the beach. The meditation of the waves brought about dreams and fantasies that stimulated her far more than her job.

Her eyes focused on Martin as he approached, bringing her out of the momentary revery with a practiced but sincere smile.

'Morning,' she spoke with a local accent, 'what can I get you?'

'Good morning,' Martin returned the smile. 'A cup of tea would be pleasant to warm my damp frame.' He comically padded the damp arms of his suit.

'Ha, nice,' she was appreciative of the humour from the stranger, most of her customers during the daytime were just so damn straight. 'It's horrible out there isn't it? I hope it clears up in time for the carnival.'

'Oh, is it carnival time?' enquired Martin with interest.

'Yeah, in a couple of days,' the waitress spoke through the chews of her gum, 'it's the seventieth anniversary this year. The council are pulling out all the stops. It's going to be a big one.'

She handed Martin a flyer with a child's drawing of clowns and fireworks. He took the piece of paper and smiled at the sight of the amateur but impassioned drawing.

The waitress stopped chewing and narrowed her eyes, 'Are you from the telly?' she asked.

'No,' Martin said, a little taken aback.

'Shame. You look familiar,' she began to pour the hot water into the cup. 'You must have one of those faces. A familiar one I mean. Milk? Sugar?'

'Uh, Milk. No sugar thanks,' he answered.

'Sweet enough hey?' she joked before turning back to the topic of the carnival. 'Floats, fireworks, marching bands, the lot. Everyone is going in fancy dress. Shame it may be a wash out.' She gazed out of the window for a moment with a glum look whilst stirring the milk into his tea. Her eyes looked lost once more as they searched for those fantasies hidden between the waves. As quickly as she faded out she snapped back to the real world with a slight shake of the head and a wry smile. 'Still, always a good turnout. One pound fifty please.'

Martin reached into his wallet and handed her a twenty pound note, apologising for not having any smaller change as he did so.

'Wow,' the waitress exclaimed as she studied the note in her hand, 'where did you get this from? Have you been raiding the savings under the mattress?'

'Sorry?' Martin asked, confused by her reaction.

'This twenty,' she held it up between their eye line, 'it's discontinued. Has been for some time.'

She handed the now defunct note back to him whilst he gave a small chuckle.

'I'm sorry, I've been away for a while. The only other thing I have is a bank card,' Martin said tapping his pockets in a symbolic gesture to show they were empty.

'Not to worry, pay on the card when you're done,' the waitress spoke reassuringly, 'in case you want anything else.'

Martin gave his thanks and, taking his tea, made his way to an empty table with a splendid view through the large windows of the storm-battered beach and withering pier.

The old man in the brown suit sipped his tea and watched the waves crashing against the sandy shoreline. His eyes ran along the pier and its all too familiar surroundings, tracing the pathways he had walked many times over as a younger man. He had seen this beach through many seasons during the years and his mind cast back to the glorious, and seemingly endless summers. The overwhelming memories forced him to close his eyes and as he reminisced he could almost feel the pleasing glow of the sun warming the back of his neck.

Martin was ten, maybe fifteen years younger as the sun

beat down on the striped tent he squatted in, wearing a plain white t-shirt to keep cool, but still keeping his trademark trilby on. He could hear the children excitedly chatting outside as they sat down with their parents in front of the tent awaiting the Punch and Judy show. Lined up beside him were his cast of hand operated stars; the crocodile, the hangman, Toby the dog, the Devil, Judy. His right hand was inserted into the puppet of the main attraction, the star of the show. With its bright red cheeks, its wide smile, its hooked nose and long chin that almost met in the middle there was no mistaking Mr Punch.

He lifted the puppet out of the booth window and into the view of his audience who screamed in delight when they saw the show starting. As the show began Mr Punch had a baby in his arms.

'Go to sleep little baby,' Mr Punch was voiced by Martin aided by a small device he placed in the roof of his mouth known as a swazzle. Through the swazzle he produced the manic and recognizable, buzz like sound.

'Waa waa,' the baby cried.

'Go to sleep little baby,' but the baby continued to wail despite the commands from a frustrated Mr Punch. 'Oh baby please be quiet.'

'Waa. Waa. Waa.'

Mr Punch ducked down behind the curtain and reappeared with a large wooden bat.

'Hush baby,' he cooed before suddenly hitting the child, wildly, with his bat. 'Smack the baby, smack the baby,' he half sang with each strike before calling out his catchphrase, 'that's the way to do it!'

'Mr Punch, what are you doing with the baby?' Judy's voice called from offstage.

'Nothing!' cried Mr Punch as he turned to the wailing infant in panic. 'Shhh, shhh'.

It refused to be quiet, and in desperation Mr Punch sat on the baby, trying to muffle the noise and hide his guilt.

Judy appeared, controlled by Martin. 'Where's the baby?' she asked as she turned to the enthralled audience. 'What's he done with the baby, boys and girls?'

The children giggled and shouted back to her. 'He's sat on him!' they cried.

'He's what?' she asked.

'He's sat on him!' they all shouted louder, pointing at Mr Punch and shrieking with laughter.

'Sat on him!' Judy slowly turned to stare at Mr Punch, holding her hands to her face she shook her head in disbelief, 'Oh Mr Punch! How could you?'

Stealing the bat from her husband, Judy began to strike him round the head. The scene of slapstick absurdity brought hysterical laughter from the children.

Extracting his revenge Mr Punch wrestled the bat from her and began to hit his wife with the cry, 'That's the way to do!'

'Ow, ow, ow,' cried Judy turning to the audience as she received the comical blows. 'Children, I think you should call the police.'

'POLICE!!' whooped the children in delight.

'Call again,' said Judy still suffering blows from Mr Punch's bat, 'they didn't hear!'

'POLICE!!!!' the children shouted even louder at the striped tent and its scene of mayhem.

Martin rested the Judy puppet over the side of the tent giving the appearance that she had laid down. Taking the Mr Punch puppet out of view he replaced him with the Constable.

'Hello boys and girls,' were the Constable's opening lines, 'what's been going on here? Who's done this to Judy?'

Whipped up into a joy of cacophonous call and response the audience screamed back at the police puppet, 'Mr Punch!'

'Who?' the Constable asked, playing stupid.

'MR PUNCH!' the audience shouted, raising their volume.

'Mr Who?' the Constable jokingly demanded.

'MR PUNCH!!!' even the parents joined in this time, egged on by the hard of hearing policeman.

'Mr Punch!' the Constable exclaimed as if this was the first time he'd heard it. 'Right then, if you see him let me know.'

On cue Mr Punch appeared behind him.

'He's behind you!' the delighted audience hollered.

No sooner had the Constable turned around than Mr Punch had disappeared, ducked down out of view.

'Where?' the confused Constable turned back to the audience. Upon doing so Mr Punch appeared again.

'He's behind you!' the audience called out, pointing in the direction of the mischievous puppet.

But again Mr Punch disappeared the moment our dim witted Constable turned to face him.

'What?' the Constable asked. 'Where?'

'He's behind you!' the audience shouted even louder as Mr Punch appeared once more.

This time the Constable turned to catch him. Not to be outsmarted Mr Punch took his bat and began to beat the Constable. The audience laughed and they all joined in with the catchphrase as he shouted with vigour through his swazzle affected voice, 'That's the way to do it!'

Once the show had finished Martin emerged from the tent and stood by its side, collecting the money from the parents. Mildred Avery and her children were regulars to Martin's seaside matinees.

'Thank you Martin,' she said as she happily handed over her money whilst her daughter stood by her side, 'the kids love it.'

'You're welcome,' he replied, 'it's a pleasure to do. And watch out for the crocodile!'

He brought a hand from behind his back to reveal a crocodile puppet that snapped its jaws as he chased Mildred's daughter until she took solace behind her laughing mother.

'I have the best job in the world,' he continued once he'd stopped his chase. 'Just as well really, I wouldn't know what else I'd do.'

They both laughed.

Martin's attention was diverted as he looked over the shoulder of Mildred, past the high spirited kids to a beautiful woman in her late thirties. Her striking blue eyes looked through a wave of auburn hair that had caught the gentle breeze and met his gaze. She smiled sweetly and looked pleased to see him return the gesture.

'Excuse me, do you mind if I sit here?'

Martin's blissful reminiscence was disturbed by a lady seemingly of a similar age to his. Her clothes were vibrant and colourful whilst her fingers and neck were adorned with a multitude of fanciful rings, necklaces and trinkets; a contrast to the grey vista of the seaside view behind her. With the way she dressed and the almost youthful playfulness in her smile her faded glamour seemed reminiscent of the seaside town itself.

Whilst Martin searched for his composure following the sudden intrusion he lost his words, but the lady sat down anyway, not waiting for an answer. She seemed so confident and relaxed, as if they'd known each other for years.

'I hope you don't mind,' she smiled a friendly beam, 'I could do with a bit of friendly company. I'm Polly.'

'Martin,' he said, at last finding his speech and a smile. 'Pleased to meet you.'

'I hope you don't mind, Martin, I'm new to the area. Just moved here a few weeks ago. I've spent so much time at home trying to get everything sorted, you know? Gas, electric, the internet. Stair lift! Ha, not quite yet. But now I'm retired it won't be long.'

Polly seemed so at ease with herself and the world around her. She spoke with a mildly husky tone that would suggest she had been a heavy smoker some years back, but it was clear she looked after herself now. Her eyebrows were carefully plucked with precision and her make up applied with well practiced and tasteful aplomb.

'Oh, I don't know,' Martin felt himself flirt, it

had been a long time since he had done that, 'you seem to have a lot more life in you just yet.'

'Thank you,' she laughed. 'I hope the fire never dies. I spent a long time getting to this age. All my life in fact. Let's just hope I can enjoy it hey? Have you reached the golden age yet?'

'Oh no,' Martin sounded a little embarrassed by such direct questioning but held it in good humour, 'not just yet. Still a few years to go.'

'And maybe more than you think if the government have their way. They keep pushing the retirement age up and up,' Polly took a sip of her tea. 'It's a wonder anyone will get there.'

'I think that's the idea,' Martin smiled. Who was this lady? In the space of a few minutes they had already covered the topics of old age and politics. 'So you're new to Stanswick? I've just moved back here myself.'

'Moved back? Where have you been?'

'I've been…away,' Martin looked uncomfortable as he searched for the words to answer without sounding rude, 'for…some years.'

'Sounds intriguing,' Polly was blunt but sincere.

'Not really,' Martin batted the answer away and steered on to a different subject, 'although if I plan on staying around I will have to look for work.' He relaxed again as the conversation continued, 'I used to be the Punch & Judy man round here many years ago. I don't suppose there's much call for a man of my skills now-a-days. It's all computer games now.'

'There is still a call for laughter and the rush of real life,' the passion resonated in her voice, 'I just hope they all understand it before it's too late.'

'I guess the closer you get to the end the more you realise just how wonderful and exciting life can be,' the old man sighed. 'They do say the sense of death approaching enriches life.'

'Who says?' Polly challenged. 'Just a load of old words to me. You don't need to be at the end to enjoy yourself.'

Her challenging nature was like a vital jolt to Martin's old and tired thoughts. When was the last time he ever questioned philosophies he'd idly made decades ago? He could feel the energy and effervescence exuding from his companion.

'Very true,' he replied, 'every experience sows a memory. And good or bad, after a while memories are all we have.'

'So let's get as many memories as we can.' Polly began to laugh at herself, 'Oh listen to us geriatrics philosophising. As if we know anything.'

Martin looked at the time on his watch, 'You'll have to excuse me,' he apologised, 'I could easily while away the hours and I'm sure we'd work out the secrets of the universe if we kept going but I've just literally got back into town. I'm sure my neglected house will need a bit of sorting.'

'But of course,' Polly spoke like she already knew this, 'don't let me hold you up. I hope you do decide to stay in Stanswick and don't go getting a job before tomorrow otherwise you won't be able to take me out.'

She gave him a wink that triggered a flattered smile to spread across his face.

'Really?' he asked, 'I would like that.'

'Wonderful. Shall we say one o'clock on the pier? We could have something to eat, maybe go for a walk?'

'One o'clock sounds fine,' Martin wasn't used to such a forward female but did not mind it one bit.

They said their goodbyes and Martin left the dazzling and fascinating Polly to her tea and cake.

'Is that everything?' the girl asked as Martin made his way to the counter to settle his bill.

'Yes thank you,' he replied as he handed over his bank card.

She took the card and smiled, 'Thank you very much Mr…' She held the card to her face to read the name on the front, but as she did so her voice began to quiver whilst the colour slowly drained from her features. '…Powell…,' she said, 'Martin…Powell.'

The girl took a step back to steady herself and in doing so she knocked a cup off the counter. It smashed in to little pieces of bone china as it hit the wood paneled floor.

'Are you okay?' Martin asked, concerned about the young girl.

'I'm fine,' she said shaking her head and handing back the card.

She got down on her knees and began to pick up the fragments of the cup that had scattered from the impact.

'Would you like a hand?' Martin asked sympathetically.

'No it's my mess. Here, please take your card. Don't worry about the charge,' her voice was strained as she tried to stay polite but inside she boiled with a mix of anger and fear.

Martin bent down to help but the girl turned to him with an assertive voice, although keeping her composure this time, 'Please! It's fine.'

'Do I know you?' Martin asked.

'I don't think so. I have one of those faces,' she replied nervously.

Embarrassed by the scene Martin bid the girl well and made his way out into the storm.

Once she was sure he was out of sight the girl left the mess on the floor and bolted to the phone. She frantically dialed a well remembered number.

'Hello, Pippa? Pippa, it's Jo. You'll never guess who's back?'

2

The house smelt damp as winter had gradually soaked through the walls. It had been untouched for the best part of a decade and its lack of occupancy had meant that no one had used the heating in order to halt the advance of the dreary seasons into the brickwork and plasterboard. The curtains had been left closed keeping the house in an eternal nighttime; ideal conditions for the rats and insects that had made it their home.

Their haven was about to be interrupted by the sound of a key sliding slowly into a rusty lock.

The entrance had grown stiff through under use and Martin pushed and pulled at the front door as he forced it open. After a few minutes of effort he forcibly persuaded the wood from the frame and gazed upon the sight of a home he had not seen in years. The light streamed through the doorway and down the hall illuminating an air full of dust particles. Martin watched their merry dance then took his first steps back into his cherished house.

'Hello home,' he softly spoke to the walls as if they were alive, 'not seen you in a while.'

He went from room to room, opening the curtains and letting the dim light from outside spill into the house, revealing the neglected condition that had been awaiting him. Each room was tidy and neat, but thick with layers of dust, turning a once cream sofa into the colour of old plasters. As he approached the kitchen he could see the table still full of letters and papers. He pulled the curtains back, coughing at the dust he disturbed, and remembered his last day here.

On the table lay a few artifacts that hinted at those times. He brushed aside a pile of old leaflets, *Debt Advice, Living with Cancer, New Chinese Takeaway Opening,* and thumbed a yellowing newspaper. Its pages had crinkled and dried with time but the print was still readable, the front page headline read: *Punch And Judy Man In Court Today.*

He looked lost in the words for a moment but was suddenly distracted from any notion of grief when he heard a noise from upstairs.

What was that?

He was the only one here. Had someone broken in? Stanswick Sands wasn't the type of place to attract squatters but perhaps times had changed. It was a new world to Martin Powell, one he needed to get used to.

Cautiously Martin crept up the stairs, treading lightly so as not to make the steps creak under his weight. As he reached the top of the landing he was back in a world of darkness and cobwebs.

'Hello? Who's there?' he called out nervously.

He tilted his head to the side and strained his

ears to listen. No reply came but he was definite he'd heard the sound of movement. Determined to discover its source he tip toed down the landing, tracing the sound to his old bedroom. He entered a still and empty room and reached down by the side of his bed. His hand found a large wooden bat that had been leaning against the wall. He was mildly surprised, firstly to have remembered it would be there but also because it was still exactly where he had left it all those years ago. This train of thought did not last long; stronger emotions currently ruled his mind. His heart thumped in his dry throat as he clenched the handle tight.

The room seemed empty, but the curtains were tall and reached to the floor. Was that a bulge in the curtains he could see? It was hard to make out through the gloom. A small twitch in the fabric confirmed his suspicions. There was someone hiding there!

Slowly Martin raised the bat behind his head, ready to swing. He wasn't a man of violence but this was his home and he was going to protect it. Wildly he swung his weapon, the curtain crumpled revealing the potential hiding place to be empty. But as it swayed from the impact a huge, black rat ran out from the behind the cotton veil. It dashed over his foot and into a wardrobe that had been left ajar on the other side of the room.

'Bloody rats!' Martin almost laughed with relief.

He would have to get some traps later as there may be more, but right now he needed to get this little blighter out of his bedroom.

Lightly walking across to the wardrobe he began very slowly to open it. He had to catch the creature by surprise, so once he had a good handle on the door he raised his bat ready for another swing. He was not going to be caught out this time. Slowly he counted in his head to three and then, with a sudden rush, threw the wardrobe door wide open.

From out of nowhere a huge, evil grin flashed in front of him as a man's head swung forward from the top of the wardrobe, coming face to face with his own. Its fixed grimace and wild staring eyes bore an unhinged expression into a terrified Martin. He stumbled backwards in fear and in the panic to flee from the crazed figure he fell, crashing to the floor. Reaching out for something to break his fall he caught hold of the curtain and pulled it from its fixings as he made his heavy landing. The curtain fell to the floor and daylight cut through the gloom, shining on the figure that swung from the wardrobe.

As his eyes adjusted Martin looked back at this potential assailant and realised it was not a wild-eyed attacker after all. Its hooked nose and protruding chin was that of a mask from a costume he once wore.

His fear turned to nostalgic recognition as he slowly rose to his feet.

'Mr Punch.'

Within a few hours the place was beginning to feel more like home. Martin had aired the house through and got the heating going again. He had spent some time dusting the place down although it was clear that many things still needed a good wash. He smiled as the night drew in and the lights went on. It was beginning to look cosy and welcoming and less like a museum of neglect and dilapidation. The phone rang as he was laying some newly acquired rat traps.

'Oh hello Frank,' he answered the phone with a genuine joy to hear the voice of the caller, 'yes thanks I'm back in now. Thanks for sorting out the electricity and the bank card, although you could have warned me the phone was set up. It gave me a terrible start. You've made it so much easier for me though; you've been so helpful. Did you know they've changed the twenty pound note?'

Sitting down on the sofa with the phone to his ear he began to idly wipe down the Mr Punch costume with a damp cloth. Propped up on the sofa like a companion it almost looked alive. The care and attention that Martin gave to it as he cleaned off the years of grime would have certainly given weight to this theory.

Beside him a cast of Punch and Judy puppets were lovingly laid out on display. Each one had been carefully taken out of an individual, velvet lined case.

'Oh you know,' he continued his conversation with Frank, 'I'm just finding my feet. The house needs a little work but nothing major. I reckon a couple of weeks before it's ready to sell.' He stopped short as Frank interjected with his comments. Martin then carried on, 'I have been tempted, I did meet a very nice lady today and the town is still so beautiful. It's carnival time again. I'd completely forgotten it would be on. Shame about the weather. I haven't really been out of the house much just yet, it feels quite amazing just to be back home.'

Holding the chin of the costume he looked down each side of the face, checking for damage.

'Seeing all my old things. It's one thing to

remember,' Martin exclaimed excitedly down the phone, 'but to see all these things after all these years. I found my old Punch costume. Remember?' His mind cast back nearly twenty years ago, 'You and your friends used to love it when I came to your birthday parties in that. I couldn't make it for your tenth birthday and you were so upset I had to call you and do the Punch voice down the phone.'

Martin picked up a small device consisting of two metal strips that were bound into an elliptical shape round a reed. This was his swazzle, the apparatus with which Martin voiced the characters from his show. He placed it into the roof of his mouth and began to talk down the phone.

'Hello Frank!' he sounded wild and crazy like any good Mr Punch should. 'That's the way to do it!'

Taking the contraption out of his mouth he regained his sensible composure with a small cough, clearly embarrassed by the reaction of Frank on the other end of the phone, 'Well you all have to grow up sometime. I guess even me.'

Martin sat back on his sofa, allowing the cushioned backrest to envelop his shoulders. This was a comfort he was not used to.

'I'm fine, really,' he reassured Frank, 'after all this time I'm so pleased the only bars I'm going to see are ones you can order a drink from.'

There was a relaxation in his own voice that he hadn't heard for years. His tone was symptomatic of a deeper sense of peace that this waking day had brought him. He had waited so long for such a day to come and it had not disappointed.

3

The sound of the cell door slamming shut felt like fingernails scraping down his soul. The crash of metal on metal echoed in his ears and vibrated through the fillings in his teeth, making him clench his jaw in agonizing pain. Shadows of the bars to his cage cast long, dark impressions along the floor and walls like ghostly, formless sentries, deaf to his anguish.

Martin sat on the bed of his cell with his head in his hands. His grief was clear as the tears ran down his cheeks. He tried in vain to sob quietly. It would be a while yet before such displays of emotion were beaten out of him.

'You're scum, Powell,' sneered a prison warden as he stood the other side of the bars tapping a baton against the steel pillars, 'you deserve everything you get.'

Martin's fear turned to inside the cell as two inmates rose from their bunks and walked towards him. A blade glinted in the hand of one of the men as he picked up the puppeteer and threw him against a wall.

The two men were both strong and rained punches with iron-like knuckles into the face of Martin. He crumpled to the floor, defenceless and catatonic with misery.

'Please,' he cried as he spat blood from his mouth.

The two criminals did not listen and rolled Martin onto his back. He kicked and shook to free himself but their might was too powerful for him. He felt his wrists being tied together behind his back with a belt.

The banging of a hammer made Martin look up. As he did so he saw a court room judge in the corner of the cell, going as red as his gown and screaming, 'Ten years! Ten years!' over and over again. Insanity crackled in the judge's voice as he repeated his sentence with disdain.

The prisoners continued to hold Martin down. He thrashed wildly, his panic bringing about a kind of fit. As his eyes rolled around the room he caught glimpses of strange images.

Two young girls, smiling, holding hands.

A gravestone.

The mad judge.

'You can be our little bitch,' one of the inmates said as he leaned close enough to Martin's ear that he could feel the warmth of his breath. It smelt like sewers.

Spittle drooled from the man's thick lips and rolled down Martin's face. The second inmate kicked him hard in the side. He let out a cry of pain and began to feel his trousers being taken off.

'That's right little man,' the prisoner's voice was

dripping with menace against the ear of his victim, 'you can be my puppet now.'

Martin looked forward at the wall and then closed his eyes tight. He felt the warmth of the prisoner's hard penis press against the back of his leg. Two thickset hands clenched his naked bum cheeks and spread them wide. He'd never felt so vulnerable in his life but he knew he could fight no more. Martin thought back to the beach and the seaside. He felt the huge, throbbing prick glide up his thigh as he recited the last Punch and Judy show he'd performed. He felt the end of the assailant's penis touch his anus, which immediately contracted in defence. As dry and unwilling as his body was he knew the force of these brutes could not be stopped.

He felt his rectum being spread wider still as, like a grotesque worm, the prisoners erection pushed and forced its way inside.

Martin woke with a shock and found himself sat upright in bed. His skin was damp and the bed sheets saturated with sweat. His bedroom was still as he wildly looked around in confusion. He panted as the adrenalin that had flooded his body took a while to subside. He was safe. He was at home.

The clock read 3:40 as he lay back on his bed, too exhausted to be concerned with damp linen. He buried his head into his pillow and sobbed. He cried for his past, the one he had suffered and the one he had missed. He quietly pleaded to any god that would listen to protect his future. And he hoped for some kind of blessing.

In the darkness of his room the Punch costume sat, propped up on a chair, and grinned an unflinching grin at the scene before him.

4

Jo had suffered a restless night of turmoil and anguish. Despite all the reassurances her friend Pippa had offered on the phone yesterday they had done nothing to alleviate the cycle of thought and fear that ran through her mind. She had decided to stop by and see Pippa before her shift at the café started, and so made an early morning call to her best friend's house.

'I never imagined he would come back,' Jo stirred her cup of tea agitatedly as she slumped in her friend's sitting room dressed in her pink uniform, ready for work.

'Come on Jo,' Pippa assured her, 'it doesn't matter. What's he going to do?'

Pippa was of the same age as Jo and they had been friends since school. She had always been the stronger one of the two so she was not surprised about Jo's reaction and current state of mind. Pippa sat down opposite her friend and dunked a biscuit into her warm beverage. Her pretty features were framed by long brunette hair that flowed in gentle waves almost reaching her bottom. She had always been the most attractive girl in her year at school, and having only left a few years ago her popularity remained in adult life throughout the town.

Jo was not convinced by her friend's blasé attitude with which she took the arrival of Martin Powell to Stanswick Sands.

'I hear what you're saying Pip,' Jo whined, 'but I just feel so awful. I was able to forget about it whilst he wasn't here, but seeing him standing there in front of me...' She trailed off for a moment, then regained her focus, 'Pip, he looks so old, so messed up. You haven't seen him. It sends shivers all over me just thinking about it.'

Jo stood up from her seat and walked to the window. On the windowsill stood a picture of the two girls when they were nine years old. The two stood together in matching yellow dresses, Pippa with a polka dot bow in her hair, holding hands. She picked up the picture and looked at the happy faces, searching for some comfort.

'Relax Jo,' Pippa watched a tear silently roll down her friend's face, 'Martin Powell is not anybody's concern any more. The person most worried about it is you.' She stood up and walked towards her distressed mate, 'And I get it, I really do. From time to time it crosses my mind just how awful it was, but that was such a long time ago. People move on. We've grown up, we have jobs.'

'You have a baby,' Jo smirked as she wiped the tear from her face.

'I have a baby. It's a different world,' Pippa held Jo for a moment in a gentle embrace. 'Now if you want shivers down your spine get Colin to have a read of this,' her tone lightened and she pulled a book out from under the coffee table.

It had the picture of a man and women, naked and interlocked in a passionate kiss on the cover. The title above the two lovers read *40 New Ways To Orgasm*.

'Really?' Jo was not convinced.

'Why not, it can't hurt,' Pippa smiled, 'I have no use for it. Haven't been in the mood since Jarred left me.'

'Why such a sexy costume for the carnival then?' Jo quizzed.

Pippa held up a black and pink corset, admiring its risqué nature.

'Nothing wrong with looking sexy,' she retorted, 'and besides I might get back into the whole dating thing once I get my sleepless nights back from little Danny.'

'Yeah yeah,' Jo mocked, 'you and your team have gone with sexy burlesque in a bid to tickle the judges fancy and win. I know you girl!'

'Moi?' Pippa faked innocence in her expression. 'I've only wanted to win this thing forever. Think I might have found a winning formula. The whole town has already been talking about my float.'

She smiled and tilted her head to one side with a compassionate smile to her friend.

'Now cheer up and relax,' Pippa said softly stroking her friend's arm, 'and if it really gets too much, well you know what to do?'

'No, what?' Jo asked.

'We're in a seaside town,' Pippa's smile grew with playfulness, 'go chuck yourself in the sea.'

5

If the town of Stanswick Sands was likened to a beached whale slowly dying on land as the surrounding environment caused it to perish, then the pier would have been its rotting tail. A decaying strip that reached back out to sea.

Martin stood on the moss covered timber that formed the pier's structure and leant against the railings. He watched the waves crash against themselves as swooping seagulls filled the air with a cacophonic chorus. The sky was grey and brooding, but the storms had held off giving the locals a reprieve from the rain. Few people had taken the chance of a dry and less windy day to venture to the pier. Among those that had were a few fishermen casting lines into the rough sea and some thrill seekers that sought amusement in the archaic attractions decorated with fluorescent lights and garish paint work.

Martin wore a long coat and hat, it had been a while since he had felt the sea breeze and he found it cold this time of year. He looked down at his watch through a pair of sunglasses and read it to be quarter past one. Polly was late for their date.

He wondered if she was going to come at all when he noticed a flash of green and purple through the crowd. Polly's coat proudly stood out as she strode with confidence to their planned meeting point.

'Polly!' Martin called.

'Martin? Why hello, I barely recognised you there,' she approached him with a smile, 'what's with the disguise?'

'What?' Martin asked.

'It's hardly weather for sunglasses,' she pointed to his face and the shades he wore.

'Oh yes,' he countered, 'I found them out when going through all my things last night. I thought I should get into the spirit of the seaside and give them an airing.'

'Shame about the weather,' Polly looked to the sky with a mild grimace, 'I hope it doesn't ruin the carnival.'

It was Martin's turn to keep the spirits high, 'Us British are made of sterner stuff than to be put off by a little bit of rain. If we were we would never get anything done!'

He made a loop with his arm and offered it to Polly. She accepted the invitation, putting her hand through the hole and round his bicep, linking arms. Together they strolled along the pier.

'There is so much joy to be had here,' Martin spoke with the enthusiasm of a tour guide, 'we have the big wheel, the dodgems.'

The pair walked into an undercover building

filled with music and flashing lights emitting from arcade machines that were lined up in rows.

'This was never really my sort of thing,' Martin raised his voice to be heard over the electronic din.

'I can't say I have ever really played any computer games,' Polly said, 'the two pee machines are as far as I go. How about that?'

Polly pointed across the room to a shooting range. Rifles were laid out on the counter in a row and behind them, on the back wall, were a series of targets. Hanging above the red and white targets were a collection of cuddly toys. Lions, tigers and bears were the prizes for the crack shot.

'How's your aim?' she asked.

'A challenge hey?' Martin tipped his hat to his date, 'I accept madam.'

Martin picked up a rifle and looked down the barrel, aiming it at the target in front of him. He shuffled uncomfortably as he tried to get a good aim but the sunglasses dimmed his view and made it hard to ensure he was set for the bull's eye. Not wanting to lose face in front of his date he took a guess and squeezed the trigger. The shot fired off but completely missed the target and instead made a hole in one of the stuffed toys hanging from the ceiling. The unfortunate lion swung in the air as its stuffing fell to the floor.

'Oops,' Polly laughed, 'I think you should try taking your sunglasses off.'

Martin smiled and reached for his shades, hesitated and put the rifle down.

'Maybe this isn't my game,' he admitted. 'Terribly sorry about the toy,' he said to the attendant, 'please let me pay for it.'

'Oh Martin you are funny,' Polly said with delight as he handed over the money. She pulled at his arm, 'Can we go on the big wheel?'

'Your request is my pleasure,' came Martin's reply as they made their way to the giant structure overlooking the sea.

The afternoon was filled with laughter and playfulness as the two tried out all the rides the pier had to offer. As they embarked on the big wheel Martin made a joke about falling off at the moment the carriage overlooked the water below. He stumbled forward and leaned out over the safety railings. Polly was initially scared but giggled when she realised it was nothing more than horseplay. The old gent got to show off his skills by hooking a duck and winning his lady a cuddly toy. He proved himself a skillful driver of the dodgems and amid screams of delight they both held their own on the waltzers. To catch their breath they sat down for a moment eating fish and chips fresh from yesterday's catch and joked about who could build the biggest sandcastle in the summer. Once they had finished their meal they strolled further along the pier, their hands met, their fingers entwined and they gently held each other's palm in a sign of togetherness that pleased them both.

'Who'd have thought there was so much fun on the pier!' Polly remarked.

'I've saved the best till last,' Martin replied as he stopped and faced an attraction. 'Polly, please let me introduce you to my particular favourite, the Maze of Mirrors.'

The lights surrounding the entrance flickered on

and off and Polly looked a little underwhelmed.

'It may not look like much,' admitted Martin, 'but just you wait until we get inside.'

He paid a bored looking attendant who barely gave them the time of day and they entered into a dimly lit room.

The maze was instantly confusing on its entrance as the mirrored walls reflected images of both them and potential passageways. Polly walked forward towards an opening but was immediately halted as she crashed into a mirror with a bang.

'Careful!' called Martin. 'Don't hurt yourself.'

Slowing her pace Polly shuffled her feet forwards with her hands outstretched. She could not trust her eyes in this place of illusion. Martin removed his sunglasses to get a better view of his surroundings.

'You could get lost in here for days,' Polly wondered in awe.

'If you really want to lose yourself,' he said, 'where better than a maze.'

'I can't work out where I'm going,' Polly called out with delight as she felt her way forward. 'Martin? Martin?'

There was no response from behind her. She stopped in her tracks. Looking round she was greeted by countless reflections of herself, each with the same concerned look on her face, but no sign of her date.

'Martin?' she called out again, her voice weak and trembling with uncertainty.

'Boo!' Martin shouted as he suddenly jumped out on her from his hiding place.

Polly shrieked and then laughed as she held on to him.

'Oh you!' she laughed. They slid into a clinch and she gazed at his face, 'It's nice to see your eyes at long last.'

'I guess some things you just have to wait for,' he quipped.

'And it was worth the wait.'

They leaned towards each other until their lips met and with a gentle but assured passion they kissed. Martin pulled her closer; his hand softly squeezed her waist, pulling her hips towards his.

As they slowly broke off from their embrace Polly looked at him with a mischievous sparkle in her eye.

'Is this where you end all your dates?' she joked.

'It's worked well for me so far,' he said with a knowing wink.

They both giggled and kissed again.

'Come on,' said Martin with rejuvenated vigour, 'my knowledge is a bit rusty but I can still find my way round.' He took her by the hand, 'Let's show you out.'

Skillfully Martin led Polly round the maze. A left, a right, an unexpected loop back round. He had to stop and think a few times, but only momentarily, and within a few minutes they emerged, blinking in the natural light.

'I can't believe it!' whooped Polly. 'You knew exactly where you were going!'

'Just one of my many useless skills,' Martin sounded bashful.

'I'm impressed,' she said kissing her hero on his cheek. 'If you'll excuse me I just need to spend a penny.'

'Good idea,' Martin thought aloud, 'I'll meet

you here.'

Of all the various states of structural and decorative decay on show along the sea front the toilets were the worst. The walls were covered in offensive graffiti, and black mould that grew in the corners spread like stubborn shadows, refusing to move regardless of the time of day. Martin walked into the portacabin marked *Gents* and was greeted with a smell of stale urine. The floor was damp with puddles collecting in the dips of the uneven flooring. Martin decided against using the shit caked toilets with their seats ripped off and leant, uselessly, by their sides and instead relieved his bladder in a urinal. He had felt his penis stir with arousal when he and Polly had kissed and he smiled to himself at the possibilities that lay before him.

As he washed his hands he found himself stood next to a large stocky man with tattoos that ran up muscular forearms. The man had a shaven head and crooked nose.

'Nice day,' Martin said politely as the two washed their hands in unison.

The other man stopped his cleaning action and turned to look at Martin with an expression like the aging man was mad.

'Not the weather,' Martin caught sight of this expression, 'it's grim outside. I'm having a nice day on the pier. I guess my mood is just colouring the day for me.'

The other man nodded in understanding and finished rinsing his hands. He then stopped and turned to face Martin, staring intently and inquisitively at him.

'Don't I know you?' he asked.

'I don't think so,' Martin smiled nervously as he shook his hands dry.

'Yes I do, yes I bloody do,' the man spoke with disbelief. 'You're Martin Powell. You used to do the Punch and Judy show here years ago.'

'You must have me mistaken,' Martin was reluctant to reveal his identity.

'Don't give me that,' the man was persistent, 'you bloody well are.'

'Uhhhh,' Martin tried to move the conversation along, embarrassed that he had been recognised by someone he didn't know, 'I'd have thought everybody would have forgotten about me by now.'

'It's been so long,' the man scratched his shaven head in bewilderment.

'Ten years,' Martin clarified.

'And it should be at least another ten!' the man's tone changed as anger began to swell in his voice.

He stepped forward into Martin's personal space until their noses met. Veins began to pulsate on his head as his features grew redder and redder.

'How do you think the town could forget about you?' he spoke whilst jabbing a thick, stubby finger into the older man's chest. 'After what you did? It makes my blood boil just to be stood in the same room as you.'

Turning the tap back on, the man scooped up some water in his hand and threw it at Martin's crotch. The water soaked into his trousers, leaving a darkened damp patch making it look like he'd pissed himself.

The man smiled a malicious smile, 'That won't be the last accident to happen if you stay around here.'

Hurriedly Martin turned and left the toilets ensuring he put his sunglasses on as he stepped back out into public. He looked ridiculous as he walked back to his meeting point with a sodden crotch but it was better than staying in the toilets to dry himself and face further wrath from his assailant.

'What on earth happened to you?' Polly was not one to politely ignore things through potential embarrassment and pointed at the dripping crotch of his suit trousers.

'Oh, just an accident with the taps,' he lied, 'come on let's go.'

'I can't take you anywhere,' she laughed as her hand slid into his and they walked away from the pier.

From the doorway of the Gents the shaven headed man watched them walk away. He balled his hands into tightly clenched fists as his rage simmered inside.

6

The date with Polly had gone very well but following the altercation with a man he did not recognise, Martin had decided it would be nice to have some company for the evening. It was a different world but history still haunted him it seemed. Grete had left a message with him that they'd like to meet up so Martin took the opportunity and invited both her and her son Kaspar round for dinner. He had always prided himself on his own ability to cook well and he enjoyed preparing the meal. If it went well maybe he'd invite Polly round for a candle lit, three course dinner. There was no better way to a person's affections than pampering them with home cooked gourmet. And in Polly's affections was where he wanted to be.

The meal had gone down a treat and Martin was delighted to see Kaspar more engaged now he didn't have his games console with him. Taking a chance, he brought out his puppets, ducked behind the sofa and reenacted his first show in over a decade. He was delighted to have his audience whoop and laugh like days of old. They both applauded as the chaotic show finished with puppets strewn across the sofa edge.

'That was brilliant Martin,' thanked Grete, 'did you like that, Kaspar?'

'Yeah,' Kaspar giggled, 'Mr Punch is funny.'

Martin emerged from behind the sofa with an ecstatic grin, pleased to have performed and been well received. He collected his puppets up and sat back on the sofa, flushed from the exuberant act of putting on his show.

'We didn't know you were a Punch and Judy man,' said a surprised Grete.

'One of the best,' Martin winked with confidence. 'How are you enjoying your stay in Stanswick? Have you been to the pier yet?'

'Not yet,' Grete replied, 'the weather has not been great.'

'Make sure you do,' he encouraged, 'I was up there today. It still has all the rides and they were just as fun as I remember. You know my old Punch and Judy tent was stored up at the pier. I haven't checked it out yet but it should all still be there. Nothing much seems to have changed.'

Tap, tap, tap.

The sound of gentle tapping came from the window. At first there were only a few raps, but then more and more as if a storm of knocking knuckles were raining against the glass.

'What's that?' Grete asked.

'Sounds like kids messing about. Just throwing stones at the window. If we ignore them they'll go away,'

Martin assured her.

Tap, tap, tap, tap, tap.

He turned to Kaspar and seized on the boy's interest in his puppets.

'Now this is Mr Punch,' he held the figure up for inspection, 'he is the star of the show. He is a very cheeky and naughty man, but he is very clever and outwits anyone he encounters.'

Tap, tap, tap, bang, tap, bang.

More stones were thrown at the window, the noises becoming louder and louder as they were thrown harder and harder. Grete looked at the window whilst a worried expression appeared on her face.

'Are you sure it's okay?' she asked. 'Shall I call the police?'

Dismissively Martin said, 'Let's not worry them,' then returned back to his tutorial with Kaspar. 'He talks in a funny voice, and we have to use a swazzle to make the voice. You do it like this.'

He took the swazzle and placed it in the roof of his mouth.

Tap, tap, bang.

'Hello little boy,' he spoke in Mr Punch's voice, 'that's the way to do it!'

Tap, tap, bang, bang, bang.

The din began to echo round the house.

Tap, bang, bang, bang!

'No one gets the better of Mr Punch,' Martin's voice started to raise in an attempt to drown out the sound of the stones, 'if he cannot outwit them then naughty Mr Punch always has his bat.'

The window began to shake as the force from

the projectiles intensified.

Bang, bang, bang, bang!

Grete grew more worried but was cut off as she said, 'I really think we should call the pol-'

'He smacks them and smacks them and smacks them,' Martin seemed unaware of his surroundings as he lost himself in his mantra of violence.

Bang, bang, bang, bang, bang, bang!

'...and smacks them and smacks them and smacks them.'

'Martin?'

Without warning Martin got to his feet and bolted to the front door. Throwing it open with force he stepped out into the street only to see some children run off down the road, laughing as they went.

'I'll get you, you little shits,' Martin called out after them.

They shouted something back, but their voices were lost to the wind.

'Are you okay?' Grete asked, worried for her new found friend.

'Bloody kids,' Martin muttered, he looked down at his feet, his voice sounded dejected. 'I'm sorry Grete. There used to be a time when they came to this house for fun.'

He closed the door and came back inside, feeling foolish for his emotional outburst. Sitting on the sofa he'd feared he'd ruined the evening but Grete just smiled and went in the kitchen to boil the kettle. The best way to cheer up an Englishman is with a cup of tea she thought.

Kaspar sat beside him and put his small arms

around the sad man's frame. The boy picked up the puppet of Mr Punch and placed it on Martin's lap.

'Don't worry,' Kaspar spoke softly to him, 'Mr Punch will get them.'

7

J. R. Park

PC Andrews rang on the doorbell again and waited. He peered through the window but could see no movement inside the house. Perhaps Martin Powell had risen early this morning. Sergeant Jack had made it clear he wanted to speak to Powell so the PC had called on him first thing this morning. He had been ringing the bell and banging on the door for the last ten minutes with no response.

He must be an early bird. These old guys don't sleep much Andrews thought as he climbed back into his car, heading back to the station empty handed.

Martin had not slept well last night and was up with the sun. He decided to invite Polly round for dinner and needed to buy more provisions for that task. He'd made it all the way to the supermarket before he realised he wasn't wearing his sunglasses. He patted down his pockets but found them all empty. Damn! He must have left them at home. He pulled his hat lower over his face to try and conceal himself a little more; he did not want a re-run of yesterday.

With a basket in hand he walked around the small supermarket selecting his items, but wary of other early morning shoppers. As another shopper got close he could feel their eyes scanning his features with a suspicious look. Did they recognise him? Or was it just paranoia? He noticed a group of people huddled and talking. Was it about him? They probably came here and had a good gossip every morning. After ten years spent in prison he would surely look different anyway. But the man in the toilets had identified him with ease. He had been such a prominent figure in the community before it all…

He turned a corner at the end of an aisle to find, blocking his path, a face he found familiar.

'Mildred?' he whispered under his breath.

'Martin?' Mildred exclaimed loudly. 'Martin Powell?'

'You must have me confused,' he tipped his hat and walked towards the checkouts. He needed to get out of here fast.

He could hear the conversation start up behind him.

'Did you see, that was Martin Powell?' Mildred spoke to a fellow shopper in her usual brash volume.

'No,' the other lady replied unable to believe it could be true.

'I swear it was,' Mildred squawked.

'What on earth does he think he's doing back here?' Martin heard the other lady say.

He approached the checkout attempting to

appear calm. The girl, sat down behind the till and ready to serve, smiled at him.

'Are you having a nice morning sir?' she asked.

Martin didn't reply, but smiled in return. He looked back at the gathering crowd around Mildred. He could no longer hear her, but he could see she was becoming visibly animated as she gesticulated and pointed in his direction.

'Shame about the weather,' the checkout girl offered as a conversation starter.

'Yes,' he nervously answered as he packed his shopping into bags.

Looking back again he watched Mildred who was now talking to a security guard.

'Do you have a loyalty card?' the girl asked.

'No, no I don't.'

He tried to keep a polite façade throughout the exchange but he was desperate to leave.

'Would you like one?' she enquired. 'I can sign you up today.'

'No thank you.'

Martin looked up again. The security guard was making his way towards them.

'That's £23.47,' the checkout assistant explained.

Martin began to panic. He picked up his shopping and pulled three ten pound notes from his pocket.

Passing them to her he said, 'Keep the change.'

'I can't do that sir,' she said.

The guard was nearly on them, he didn't have time for protocol.

'It's fine,' he said and without waiting for an answer he turned to make his quick exit.

As he turned he stumbled into another girl dressed in a supermarket uniform, the jolt causing his shopping to swing in his hand. A jar of cranberry sauce fell from the top of the bag and smashed onto the floor leaving a sticky mess of glass and red jelly. Martin's eyes immediately caught sight of the girl's name badge. It read *Pippa*.

At first startled by the impact Pippa apologised to the man she had walked in to. As she looked up at his tired and withered face she caught a glimpse of someone she knew from her past.

'Mr Powell?' she asked.

'Excuse me sir,' the assertive voice of the security guard boomed behind them as he reached the checkout.

Pippa looked at the old man. Like a confused animal caught in the headlights of an oncoming juggernaut he seemed rooted to the ground, unable to move as he watched his certain doom grow ever closer. She glanced across to the security guard and a multitude of expressions quickly flitted across her face. First she looked puzzled, trying to understand what was happening in this situation. Puzzlement was quickly replaced with alarm. Her face turned white and she began to scream in panic.

Martin snapped back to his senses as the girl in front of him shrieked. Without another second to waste he bolted out the door. He looked back as he made his swift exit but no one followed.

The security guard and shoppers had crowded

round the distressed Pippa trying to calm her down. Martin Powell could wait.

'Pippa,' a checkout assistant said as she placed a comforting arm around her, 'Pippa, you are going to be okay.'

8

'You are going to be okay.'

'I know I will,' Pippa had calmed down once she had been driven back home and to the safety of the family house.

She was sat in the living room with her parents, who concerned, had taken the day off work to rally round and talk with her. They nursed cups of luke-warm tea in their hands as they tried to make sense of what had happened and what to do next.

Pippa had surprised herself at her own reaction in the supermarket, 'Jo said she saw him at the Minstrel but it was so different seeing him stood in front of me. It was just such a shock, you know?'

'I bet it was,' her father was seething with anger. 'I've got a mind to-'

'Dad. It's not needed,' Pippa cut in. 'You and Mum have been great to me all this time. You've really looked after me since Danny was born. When I was pregnant I didn't know what to do and you were both so good. You don't need to do any more.'

Her father stood up to release some of the adrenalin that had begun to build through his anger, 'Well the same goes with Powell as what I said about that good for nothing Jarred. Jarred disappeared as quickly as you could say *baby*. If I was to ever catch sight of him.'

Her father was very protective and still held a simmering grudge over the way Jarred had bolted the moment Pippa found out she was pregnant. She hadn't told her parents straight away so they couldn't understand when he just split from their daughter and left town. Once she had come clean about the truth the boy was long gone despite her dad's best efforts to hunt him down.

'Your Dad means well honey,' her Mum chipped in, 'you just keep out of the way of that Martin Powell whilst he is here. God knows why he ever came back.'

'I guess we all have to go somewhere,' Pippa found herself saying.

'Are you sympathizing with him?' her father barked.

'No…kind of…I don't know,' his arrival had thrown her world upside down. Pippa did not know how she felt.

'Well I spoke to the manager and he won't be welcome round the supermarket again,' her father's reassurances sounded more like threats than words of comfort.

Pippa's mother knew that things could get out of hand if the two were left to bicker and so she brought the conversation onto more light-hearted topics.

'Have you organised a baby sitter for the carnival yet?' she asked. 'It is tomorrow night after all.'

'Yes that's all sorted.'

Her mother felt bad they hadn't been able to help, 'You know we would normally do it but we got such a good deal for our holiday we just couldn't turn it down.'

'Although I'm not so sure we should be going in light of recent events,' he father remarked through his bushy, black beard.

'Don't even think about staying home,' Pippa could bark as well as her father. 'You guys deserve a break. The baby sitter is sorted and I'm going to win first prize at the carnival. Our float is so good and we've spent all year working on it.'

'We're both so proud of you,' her mother was always there to pay a complement to her cherished child.

'And Jo will be around with me as well. Although I'm a bit worried about her. She seems to be taking this much harder than me,' Pippa looked concerned at the thought of her best friend.

'Look after that girl,' her Dad's tone warmed, 'she's always been there for you.'

'I will Dad,' she replied with a smile, 'you go have a good holiday. I'll win the carnival. I'm going to be okay.'

She gave them both a long, affectionate embrace, momentarily eclipsing the history of fear and worry she had endured.

9

J. R. Park

The light was low, the room only illuminated by the candles that stood in the centre of the dining table. Surrounding them were the products of Martin's cooking based labour. He had taken to cooking today with a great zeal, spurred on by last night's successful dinner, but also as a way to try and blot out the terrible events that happened this morning. He would right the awful scene by doing something positive, cooking Polly the most amazing meal she'd ever tasted. As well as the food being exquisite he'd ensured the house was clean and the finest cutlery was used. He'd also made an effort with himself, wearing his most expensive suit and purple, silk tie.

'You certainly know how to impress a lady,' Polly remarked.

She had come dressed equally as glamourous in a silk, light blue dress. Her necklace created a web like pattern of chains and jewels across her chest whilst her earrings were made of blue feathers that hung down from her ears and shimmered gently in the candlelight. Her lipstick accentuated her pout as she spoke each word.

'My pleasure,' he said as he joined her at the table.

Martin's guest looked at the spread laid out on the table and took in the rich aromas that made her salivate with anticipation.

'It smells beautiful,' Polly said appreciatively, 'can you pass me the potatoes.'

'Of course,' Martin passed her a bowl of new potatoes that glistened with a coating of butter. 'Apologies about the lack of cranberry sauce.'

'We've got everything else,' she took hold of the potatoes and spooned three onto her plate, 'I'm sure it won't be missed.'

Polly carefully put the bowl down and looked directly into Martin's eyes.

'I had such a lovely time yesterday,' she told him.

'So did I,' he agreed with a self satisfied smile, 'thank you for coming.'

'No more accidents with the taps?' she joked.

'Ummm…no. I have been okay since,' he laughed.

'And are you glad to be back?' she asked.

Martin leant back in his chair and took a moment to reflect. He watched the flames of the candles flicker for a few seconds before responding.

'I wasn't sure what it was going to be like if truth be told,' he started slowly in his speech, pondering each word before he released it from his lips. 'The place is still as beautiful as ever, even if the weather has been so rotten. My plan was to sell the house and move on, but it's such a nice place.'

'Such a nice house too,' Polly added.

'I've had this house for thirty years,' he looked around the room. 'So many memories, so many happy memories.'

'I bet the house is worth a pretty penny,' Polly remarked.

'Oh yes, I expect it's worth a lot more than what I bought it for,' he chuckled.

'But there isn't really a price you can put on memories is there?' she philosophised.

'No, not at all.' Martin rose to his feet and presented a bottle to his dining companion, 'More wine?'

She smiled and he poured her another glass full.

'The truth is, Polly,' Martin continued when he sat back down, 'I was all set to leave. Ready to sell up and make a new start somewhere else. But then no sooner had I set foot in Stanswick again than I find a reason to stay.'

'Oh?' she asked. 'And what is that?'

'The most wonderful reason of all,' he answered, 'I met you pretty Polly. I met you and all my doubts and cynicisms melted away. You make me feel like I'm alive. Just at the moment when I was horrified something inside me might have died you proved that I was wrong. You proved that life could be exciting and fantastic again. You proved things can start over. You proved I could still love.'

'Oh Martin.'

She felt tears well in her eyes at the outpouring

of this emotion and her heart gently cantered in her bosom. Their hands met and clinched, each finger interlocking around the next. Then, with their eyes fixed on the heavens they saw in each other, they leant across the table to kiss. Their lips tingled for the sensation of the other's to be pressed against them.

Their tender moment was interrupted when, without warning, a shattering sound pierced the air. The window smashed in an explosion of glass as a brick flew through it at speed. The make shift missile landed in the middle of the table narrowly missing the two lovers. As it crashed amongst the servings of a romantic meal it smashed plates and threw gravy in the air, splashing Martin and Polly dressed in their finest dinner wear.

'Are you okay?' Martin asked a shocked looking Polly.

She tried to wipe the smear of food from her clothes but they had already stained.

'Oh dear,' she said in horror, 'look at me!'

She held her arm up to reveal a cut just below the elbow. A piece of flying glass had sliced her forearm!

Anger swirled in his stomach. He could put up with the abuse that came his way, but Polly didn't deserve this. How dare they bring her into it! How dare they hurt her! He turned to the sofa where his Punch costume had been drying from its earlier cleaning. Perched against its outstretched hand rested the wooden bat. The costume's face grinned, unflinchingly at Martin as if it offered him the weapon with an evil smile. Angrily he took hold of the bat and ran to the front door, prepared to take on whoever might be out there.

'You fucking bastards,' he shouted as he made

his way onto the street, 'I'll get you, you bastards!'

But as he stepped out into the cold air the road appeared deserted. No one was there. Whoever had thrown the brick must have run off or be hiding. Martin didn't care if they were still in the street or not, if they were hiding he was going to show them a thing or two. He swung the bat around wildly through the air, screaming as he did so.

'Come on you cowards,' he screamed as if possessed by a nature far more malevolent that his own, 'I'll rip your heads off! Come and face me! I'll beat you to a pulp! I'll kill you all, you hear me? I'll kill you all! You destroyed my life once. Are you determined to do it again? Is that what you want? I'll destroy yours! Just leave me alone. Leave me alone!'

He broke into a sob as he continued to swing his weapon and didn't notice Polly as she came out to comfort him. Before he realised she was there he felt his bat strike her on the shoulder, knocking her to the ground. The sickening feel of his weapon hitting his lover immediately drained his anger from his body, leaving him with a gut wrenching remorse.

'Polly! Polly! Are you okay?' he cried in a weak and pathetic voice.

He took her by the arm and helped her to her feet. His head span with adrenalin and his ears rang as he tried to centre himself, to give his lover the attention she needed.

'I'm so sorry,' he pleaded to her, 'I've been hounded by some yobs for a few days. I'm so sorry.'

'I don't know what's going on,' Polly said as she straightened herself out, 'but I think I'll be going home.'

'Polly,' he called out after her as she stormed off, 'please let me walk you.'

'No,' she called back angrily, 'I'll be safe enough. More safe than I would be if I stayed here. Goodnight!'

As Martin watched her walk down the street he knew it would be useless to follow. She didn't look back once, and when she was out of sight he turned to the house, went inside and slumped on the sofa. He looked at the mess around the room and tears began to trickle down his cheeks once more.

Not Polly as well, he thought. Please not Polly. I can't lose it all. Not again.

Sleep began to drag him from consciousness as the sorrowful man fell forward onto the sofa. He crashed into the soft cushions and disturbed the Punch costume that slipped down the back rest.

Its arm fell on top of Martin's head, softly, like it was offering him comfort. As if it was the only friend he had.

10

Martin couldn't remember going to bed but that's where he found himself when he woke up with a start. Looking around the room it was still nighttime and the rain rapped gently against the window. As usual his skin was damp with sweat, a symptom of the nightmares he had endured. But this time it was different. The room wasn't as still as it normally was. The shadows seemed to restlessly undulate from the corners of his eyes and the air felt thin in his lungs. As he came to he could hear an incessant clicking sound, over and over. He strained to listen through the ringing of silence realising it wasn't a clicking at all. No, this was laughing.

It was faint but sounded like it was in the house, like it was coming from downstairs.

Martin slowly crept down the dark staircase, the laughter growing louder and more distinct as he got closer to its source. He made his way through the living room and noticed the bat by the sofa. He picked it up for protection and immediately felt more comfortable.

The brown bat looked grey in the dark light but the end seemed black. As Martin studied the end he watched the blackness drip from the bat onto the floor. It ran like liquid, pooling on the carpet. He dipped his fingers into the puddle and, bringing them to his nostrils, he smelt the metallic aroma of blood. Looking up he noticed the same black blood had made a trail, snaking across the floor and into the reception room. He thought it strange that no fear entered his mind as he followed the gory trail and found Pippa lying dead on the floor. Her eyes had rolled back and blood trickled from her mouth. He tried to feel shocked, to feel disgusted at the sight before him but his emotions remained Prozac flat.

He eyed the bat in his hand.

This was the weapon that killed the poor girl. The weapon that I am holding, he thought.

Instinctively he dropped the bludgeoning device as if the carved wooden stick was the evil somehow responsible for the death of the girl that lay before him.

The laughter grew louder and more manic as it began to echo in his head. Turning his back on the corpse he followed the sound of the crazed hysterics. Was he going mad? Was that the laughter of Mr Punch?

Making his way into the kitchen he found a wooden chest positioned in the middle of the floor. Martin had never seen this chest before and approached it with caution. Kneeling down he pulled back the latch that kept it shut and slowly opened the lid. The laughter grew louder as the lid came back.

Inside the chest his Punch and Judy dolls were neatly packed away, one on top of the other. As he eyed the expertly carved puppets the laughter grew louder still and shook through his brain. Pain surged across his forehead. He clenched his cranium and fell to the floor, his legs giving way under the strain of the torture that pounded inside his skull.

Just at the moment it became almost too unbearable the laughter seemed to melt away, being replaced by a chant of a hundred voices that looped round and round.

'Make them pay, make them pay, make them pay,' the voices chanted with vengeful abandon.

The window beside him smashed and glass fragments rained down around him. This time it was not a brick however as he watched the missile continue its trajectory across the room and roll onto the floor. This time it was Polly's severed head! Her lips were still bright red with this evening's lipstick and there was no mistaking those blue, feathered earrings.

'Make them pay, make them pay,' the chanting grew louder.

He tried to get to his feet but found all strength had vanished from his body. He turned his gaze back to the chest and watched, wide-eyed, as the puppets stood up, one by one, and began to walk towards him.

As they got closer he could see their mouths moving, mimicking the chants.

'Make them pay, make them pay.'

The puppets formed a circle around their paralysed master. He tried again to stand, to thrash his arms, to make a sound, but nothing was forthcoming. All he could do was watch as the Punch puppet climbed out of the chest and walked with uneven steps towards him. It climbed up on his body and along his chest until it met his gaze, eyeball to wooden, painted eyeball.

'Make them pay, make them pay,' the others chanted louder and louder.

The Punch puppet opened Martin's mouth wide and, head first, began to crawl in. Martin gagged and choked as his breathing was cut short whilst the mischievous character of make believe dragged itself down his throat.

The phone bellowed across the house and freed Martin from his horrific vision. He sat upright in bed and gasped large breaths of air. He picked up the phone receiver and glanced at the clock. It read half past nine.

'Hello?' Martin answered.

'Hello Martin, it's Polly,' came the unexpected but familiar voice.

'Polly!' he gasped again. 'I'm so sorry about yesterday. Are you okay?'

His apology stumbled over itself as he tried to get it out before she might hang up.

'Look Martin,' she spoke calmly but with authority, 'I'm sorry about last night as well, I shouldn't have left you like I did. I used to be in a violent relationship and your outburst brought back some horrific memories.'

His stomach contracted as he understood her reaction, 'I'm so sorry. Please forgive me. It's been strange for me coming back and getting used to life here. I should keep my temper under control. You must know that I would never intentionally hurt you.'

'Everything happened so fast yesterday,' she explained sympathetically, 'I've been up all night thinking about how badly I acted. You clearly needed me and I shouldn't have left. Why don't we meet up at the pier today?'

'That would be good,' he swallowed a lump in his throat.

'Shall we say twelve o'clock?' Polly suggested.

'Twelve o'clock it is.'

This was the news Martin had hoped for. Mistakes can happen, people can do bad things, but people can also be forgiven. They could be offered another chance. He felt himself weep a little, like he had over the last few years, but this time it was for a very different reason.

11

J. R. Park

It was the day of the carnival and the town was buzzing with excitement and preparations. Martin soaked up the atmosphere of the townsfolk as he made his way to the pier. This was the Stanswick Sands he remembered. He heard his name being called across the street and looked around, fearful following the events of the last few days. To his pleasant surprise he saw the pretty figure of Grete innocently waving at him from the entrance to the pier. He crossed the street and bounded towards her.

'Hello Martin,' she called out, 'how are you?'

'Hello Grete, I'm fine,' he responded to her greeting, 'I'm just taking in the local scenery. You've found the joys of the pier then?'

'Oh yes,' Grete was always so nice and friendly, 'it really is a lovely place. And thank you so much for the other night. Is everything okay?'

'Yes it's fine,' Martin brushed her concerns aside with a little lie, 'haven't had any more trouble. Just kids messing about.'

Kaspar came running up to his mother excitedly pleading.

'Mum, mum, can I go again?' he begged.

'Of course you can, but afterwards you're going to take me on the big wheel, right?' Grete instructed as she handed her son some coins.

Kaspar agreed and dashed off to the entrance for the Maze of Mirrors. The two adults watched him run with an excitable charge and they smiled for his youth.

'You were right about the Maze of Mirrors,' Grete explained, 'Kaspar loves it. I think he's been in five times now.'

Martin gave a triumphant grin, 'Like I always say, they can make computer games as realistic and complicated as they like but nothing beats a good old fashioned bit of real life fun.' He turned back to Grete, 'If you have time later on today I could show you my old Punch and Judy tent. I could give Kaspar a taste of the real British seaside.'

'Kaspar so loved the puppets, but our day is quite full,' she said apologetically.

'What about the end of the day,' Martin persisted, eager to get back behind the tent and perform, 'straight after the carnival?'

'Really?' Grete sounded genuinely pleased. 'If it's no problem.'

'It's no problem. My old storage room is here on the pier. The tent may need a little cleaning but it's all still here,' he explained. 'I'll get it set up. It would be a nice way to end the evening for the little boy. Meet me here.'

He pointed to the ground they stood on.

'Okay, it's a date,' Grete winked.

'Excellent. Speaking of dates I have one shortly, with a very pretty lady,' Martin looked at his watch and it read one minute to twelve.

The two said their goodbyes. Grete went to wait for Kaspar at the exit of the Maze of Mirrors whilst Martin took a spot to view the waves rolling gently in the surprisingly mild weather.

He didn't have to wait for long as Polly arrived in a flourish of blue and purple velvets, unusually punctual. He waved to her and beamed as he mused over her beauty.

'Polly,' he called as she approached, 'thank you so much for meeting me, you look lovely today. Would you like a-'

His offer was cut short when her face changed to a scowl and her palm slapped him, hard across the face. Martin was taken aback and looked at her, open mouthed and dumb founded; his face glowing red from the contact.

'What is the meaning of this?' she demanded as she threw a local newspaper down at his feet.

The front page had a picture of Martin Powell on it and the headline beside the unflattering and out of date portrait read *Convicted Paedophile Returns*.

Jo held the same edition of the newspaper in her hand as she stormed frantically round Pippa's living room, overwhelmed and pulling at her hair.

'You said they would forget about it!' she

whined to Pippa. 'That no one here was bothered! This article seems pretty bothered.'

She threw the newspaper to the floor, disgusted to look at it any more.

Pippa was calm and collected, 'I'll admit I was shocked to see him and I may have over reacted but this is tomorrow's chip paper. Forget about it.'

Her calming demeanor had no effect on her best friend who continued to pace up and down the length of the room.

'Forget about it?' Jo cried. 'It's such a mess. So long ago, so much trouble and for what? How much did we take? Thirty, forty quid?'

'Forty quid,' Pippa answered coldly, 'and we didn't even spend it! You went and burned it didn't you? Saying you felt so guilty.' Her voice still held tones of resentment for something so historic.

'And the guilt has been eating away at me for all these years,' Jo knew this day would come, 'I wish we had just fessed up to our parents about stealing the money when Mr Powell caught us.'

Pippa sounded angry as she recounted the past. 'He caught us! He didn't have to threaten to tell our parents!' She took her friend by the arms and guided her to a seating position on the sofa, her voice soft and gentle once more, 'Look it was bad, I know. But we were young. How were we to know what would happen? It's too late to go back now.'

Jo nodded and looked at her feet, ashamed of herself and unable to look Pippa in the eye. Pippa rose to her feet and picked up the paper that had been tossed to the floor, glancing over the article.

'He's here,' she said, 'but the paper is still siding with us, and that means so is the town.' She began to read the article in a mocking tone, 'Poor Phillippa Starr was startled when she came face to face with Martin Powell. Poor. Phillippa. Starr.' She hung on every word, over emphasizing the pronunciation of each syllable until it sounded ludicrous.

Jo giggled at her friend's comic interpretation and wiped away the moisture from her cheeks. From the next room a baby began crying. Pippa left Jo for a moment then came back holding her son in her arms. She cooed and spoke softly to him.

'Did we wake you Danny? Are you hungry?' She turned back to Jo, 'Forget about it. We'll have fun tonight at the carnival and tomorrow no one will care about Martin bloody Powell.'

'Yeah you're right,' Jo sounded more cheery by the minute. 'I have to finish work first.'

'You have a shift tonight?' Pippa asked.

'Nothing I could do about it. But I'll be out afterwards.'

Pippa cradled her child and sat next to her friend, giving her a reassuring smile.

'Good. Everyone will have a great time at the carnival and this sorry mess will all be forgotten,' she purred. 'Everything will be fine.'

'Everything is not fine!' Polly screamed to Martin as they stood arguing on the pier. 'We go out and have fun, I let you kiss me. You lose it last night and I forgive you. I come to meet you here and see this on the front page of the local paper! Now I know where you've been for the last ten years. Prison!'

'Polly you have to listen to me,' he pleaded, 'I was set up by a couple of kids.'

She turned and began to walk away, unwilling to listen, but this time Martin did not just watch her storm off and instead followed behind.

'Listen,' he implored, 'I caught them stealing some money from me on the beach. I chased them off and threatened I would speak to their parents. The next thing I know I have an angry mob outside my house and the police come and arrest me saying I had sexually abused the girls. Polly…'

She continued to march on, uninterested in his cries for innocence. His frustration grew, if only she would give him a chance and listen. Out of desperation he held her arms and stood in front of her, blocking her path.

'Please listen. Please believe me,' he begged, 'the town had made their mind up. I didn't stand a chance. I would never have done such a thing. I was hap-'

'Get off me Martin!' she screamed.

Her protests where loud enough to attract three young men that were walking by. To Pete, Jordan and Paul the pier was their territory and all the young kids in the town knew it. It seemed this old man needed to be educated.

'Are you okay, Miss? Is he bothering you?' Pete asked, sounding concerned but really just grateful for a bit of action.

'Hey,' said Jordan pointing at Martin, 'I recognise you. You were on the front of the paper this morning.'

The third member of the gang, Paul, stepped close to Martin and began pushing him violently.

'Yeah,' Paul scoffed as he pushed Martin clear of Polly, 'you're that paedo Punch and Judy guy. Come back to find some more kids have you?'

These men did not want to listen to anything Martin had to say and he knew it would be futile to argue. Abandoning Polly where she stood for her own safety Martin walked down the pier, away from his aggressors.

'Where you going, paedo?' Paul called out as they followed.

They shouted abuse and giggled to themselves as they began to spit at him. Drawing phlegm from the back of their throats with exaggerated effort and spitting the disgusting mixture of snot and saliva onto Martin's back. The vile projectiles stuck to the back of his suit jacket and slowly dribbled down the brown wool to the vocal delight of the trailing yobs. Unable to withstand much more of this humiliation Martin made a break for it and ran across the pier into the arcades. The men gave chase but lost him amongst the rows and rows of machines. They split up, each looking down an aisle to try and flush him out from his hiding place.

'Come out, come out wherever you are,' mocked Pete as they systematically took one aisle at a time.

Crouched beside a fruit machine Martin knew his hiding place would very quickly be discovered. All three of the lads were looking for him, which meant the exit was clear. They weren't the brightest of sparks, which gave him an idea.

'There he goes,' shouted Pete as he pointed to the old man.

Martin dashed out through the exit and headed for a place he knew all too well, the Maze of Mirrors. He sprinted past the attendant who began yelling at the unlawful entrant. The man's voice going even higher and frantic when Pete, Jordan and Paul ran through as well. Despite his annoyance the attendant seemed reluctant to move from his comfortable seat. When he realised none of them were coming back to pay he gave up his verbal threats and went back to watching the small television that was plugged into his booth as if nothing had happened.

Martin collided with a mirrored wall on his rushed entrance to the gloomy but loved attraction. Standing back a bit he shook some sensibility into his panicked mind.

Come on now you stupid old fart, he thought, concentrate.

Looking over his shoulder he saw the three hoodlums enter the dimly lit maze. He had to keep moving. Cautiously but with skill he made his way through the puzzle, just as he'd shown Polly. Keeping to the centre of the path he picked his way through using a combination of muscle memory and tracing a map in his mind. Behind him he could hear his would be pursuers not getting on so well.

As soon as Pete, Paul and Jordan entered the attraction they made the same mistake as Martin and slammed straight into a mirrored wall. The three piled up on top of each other, looking like a comical beast made of thrashing limbs.

'Get off me,' shouted Jordan to the rest as he lay at the bottom of the pile.

'I hate this place,' protested Pete.

'He's over there,' shouted Jordan as he got to his feet.

They ran at Martin but only went a few metres before crashing hard into another wall. The image they saw had only been a reflection.

Pete held his nose in pain.

'Where is he?' demanded Jordan.

'Where are we?' asked Paul, confused as to which way they should go and which way they came.

He made a step forward and instantly head butted another wall.

'Owww,' he cried.

With each step they made they seemed to be either hitting into a wall or each other.

Bang, crash, thud, owwww!

Jordan shouted in frustration, 'Seriously, what the fuck?!'

'Get on your knees and crawl,' Pete suggested.

They slowly got to their knees and began to crawl forward, inch by inch. It was a preposterous sight to watch these grown men reduced to such a ridiculous measure.

'This floor is gross,' Jordan complained, 'I've put my hand in something…'

'What?' Pete was not in the mood for this level of moaning. They may be crawling like babies but they didn't need to act like them too.

'Owwwww!' exclaimed Paul as he cracked his

head against another wall.

It didn't take long for Martin to reach the exit and escape to freedom. The sounds of the others were still echoing through the maze.

'I think I can see daylight,' shouted Pete, 'that must be the exit.'

'When I find that old bastard!!!' Jordan shouted, egged on by the possibility of escape.

Thud!

'Owwwwww!' moaned Paul as he smacked his head once more.

Martin could hear they were close. By luck they had stumbled the right way and it wouldn't be long before they were out and after him again. As fast as he could run, he raced off the pier and down the street, heading towards town. Martin looked behind him, his pursuers weren't in sight, but he knew they would be hot on his heels soon. As he reached the town centre he desperately looked for a way to get out of view. Without thinking he dived into the nearest building hoping to hide from Pete, Paul and Jordan.

He rushed through the door and closed it behind him, turning to see a lively group of patrons, all enjoying a Saturday afternoon drink. He quickly realised he had walked into the George, the local pub. He straightened his clothing and caught his breath. He had no choice but to try and blend in, hide in the background as a visitor for the carnival. The photograph on the paper was not a great likeness as it had been taken ten years ago so he had a chance. It was better than going back outside and getting chased down by those three thugs.

Martin made his way further into the pub. As he did so he caught glances from patrons. Did they recognise him? He focused his eyes straight on the bar, trying to act as normal as possible, but from the corners of his eyes he could see people nudging each other and pointing. Slowly the volume of chatter began to lower as one by one the Saturday afternoon revelers stopped talking and watched Martin make his journey. By the time he reached the bar the pub was silent.

Trying to maintain a pretence of normality he ordered a drink.

'Good morning,' he said to the smiling barman, 'a pint of lager please.'

The barman nodded and began to pour the pint. His service was friendly and courteous, at odds with the staring crowd.

When the pint had been poured the barman held the full glass in front of him and, not breaking eye contact with Martin, began to draw phlegm from his throat. Slowly he let the globule of saliva drip from his mouth and into the drink, its mucus matter mixing with the foamy head of the pint.

'That's all you're fit for, sir,' the barman mocked as he slammed the glass down.

The silence in the room was replaced with little sniggers and chuckles from the crowd of customers that watched this exchange, transfixed.

The barman leant closer and with a quiet but stern voice said, 'I suggest you leave.'

On cue some of the men stood from their seats and took a few paces towards Martin.

He turned to these men and held out his palms as a sign of peace, 'I don't want any trouble.'

'Then you best get the hell out of here,' one of the men threatened, 'and don't stop until you've left town.'

The man didn't wait for a reply and swung a large fist at Martin. It hit him square in the mouth, cutting his lip and knocking him to the floor. The crowd jeered and applauded as a number of others helped to pick Martin up and threw him out the door of the George. He landed hard onto the wet concrete outside.

'There's the fucker,' the shout came from Pete.

The three had escaped the attraction and wanted revenge.

'Fucking paedo,' Paul shouted as he kicked Martin in the ribs.

The fifty year old lay helpless on the floor as the three men punched and kicked him, their assault punctuated with insults. Through the legs of his attackers Martin saw two policemen stood a few metres away.

'Help me!' he called out to them.

The two officers looked in his direction, as he lay bloodied on the pavement. One stepped forward but was halted by the other. He put his hand on his colleague's shoulder and Martin saw him whisper something. Drinking the coffees in their hands and with smirks on their faces the officers held back and watched the violent spectacle as fist after fist laid into the old puppeteer, surrounded by a baying crowd.

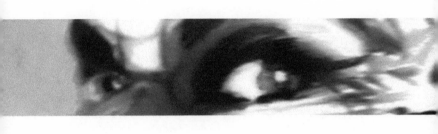

12

The guards looked on as his head was held, vice-like, in the hands of Bic. Bic was a brute of a man and for the safety of the public he would never leave prison again. He worked out in his cell every day and had grown huge as a result. Testosterone ran rampant through his body and needed outlets from time to time. The guards knew exactly what they were doing when they put Martin in his cell, and they sat back to watch the unfolding spectacle.

'Going to make you look pretty,' Bic spoke with the voice of a simpleton.

Martin tried to shout, but as he opened his mouth Bic squeezed his cheeks together, trapping it into an enforced O shape. The blonde, straw-like wig began to slip down Martin's head and rested against his ear as the brute smeared lipstick onto his victim's lips. He turned his head in defiance but all this achieved was to smudge the red make up further round his face. The guards howled with laughter at his clownish appearance.

'Looking good Powell, you nonce,' one of them joked making a thumbs up sign.

Martin wriggled in the clutches of Bic as he protested against this humiliation.

'You're going to make me feel warm and nice,' Bic spoke softly and tenderly, 'all night.'

Martin knew what was coming, and knew he would be powerless to prevent it, but he still fought. In a few months he would have all his self-respect and dignity beaten out of him. He would learn that if he didn't fight and just laid down to take it then the tears in his rectum would not be so great. They would heal by the time he was subjected to the same torture again and he wouldn't scream in agony every time he needed a shit.

He would also suffer less bruising, especially to the face. But these were lessons yet to be learnt. For now he fought, and as Bic got frustrated he punched. He punched, he kicked, he threw Martin against the cell bars and beat him with the empty coffee mug, handed to him by one of the on looking wardens.

As his trousers were ripped from his legs blood trickled down his thigh. The struggle had torn open the scabbed wounds from their previous meeting and brought him a fresh feeling of pain. Bic threw him onto the bed and tied his hands behind his back using his own trousers.

The blood felt warm as it leaked from his ass but despite the pain he was thankful that the liquid might act as some kind of lubricant and offer mild relief to the internal bludgeoning that was to follow.

These haunted memories that he'd done his best to forget tormented him as he lay in a holding cell at Stanswick police station. He lay on the bed, bruised, and recounted every attack from prisoners and wardens that he had been subjected to over the last decade. Every humiliation he endured for being labeled a paedophile in a population of the most vile and violent men in the country.

He had prayed every day for the day of his release. But when that day came and he headed home he found no comfort in this town. Maybe it was time to move away. Change his name and start again.

His meditations of suffering were cut short as the cell door opened.

A police officer put his head through the door. 'Wake up Powell,' he commanded, 'the sergeant wants to see you.'

J. R. Park

13

J. R. Park

The police station was as run down as the rest of the town. It was a quiet town in general and what little money came in to the local council was not handed out for the up keep of the station. Martin was led out of the cell and into the office of Sergeant Jack. It was a small office with enough room for a desk, two chairs and one solitary filling cabinet. Despite its size it was clean and tidy. The office had a large window that overlooked part of the town and through it Martin noticed the sky growing darker. He could sense a storm coming.

'Looks like you've had a busy day,' Jack remarked as he offered Martin a seat.

Sergeant Jack stroked his well-groomed, ginger beard as he watched Martin sit down. He was a fair man but his main interest lay in keeping the lawful peace to Stanswick Sands.

'I didn't do anything,' Martin answered back.

'That's not what I've been told.' Jack began to count the offences one by one on his fingers, 'Accosting a woman in the street and frightening her to death. Causing a disturbance on the pier. Dodging a fare for the Maze of Mirrors. Causing a fight in the George. Impressive list for an afternoon's work.'

'It's not like that,' pain shot up Martin's bruised cheek as he spoke.

'Oh really?' Jack leant forward on his chair. 'What is it like?'

'They started on me,' he was tired of defending himself, 'and your lot did nothing to help.'

'Listen Martin,' Jack calmly spoke with the relaxed, yet authoritative air of a doctor, 'my men don't like you. This town doesn't like you. Have you seen the paper this morning?'

'Unfortunately yes. They shouldn't be printing things like that. I have rights.'

'Your rights don't seem to mean much here,' Jack spoke it like it was. He regarded Martin for a while, 'You've got a lot of bottle, returning, but it's ill placed courage. I heard you were back and I have been worried. I sent one of the guys to check on you the other day but you weren't in. According to the paper you were out causing a disturbance in the supermarket. What are you doing here?'

His question was of genuine concern, both for the town and for the former convict.

Martin shrugged, 'Where else can I go?'

'We live on an island,' Jack responded, 'plenty more seaside towns.'

'I just need to sort my house out and get it sold,' Martin spoke with more assertiveness this time, he had spent his time in the cell planning his next move, and that was one of escape, 'this town has already taken everything I hold dear. A few weeks and I'll be gone.'

'Good,' Jack was pleased with the answer, 'you'd better be. I've spoken to Frank, he'll be down to see you soon and help you along your way, I know he's been helping you out. We'll take you back home.'

Sergeant Jack stood up and held the door open for Martin. They left the office and made their way outside where they got into a police car.

'My advice,' said Jack as he started the engine, 'is to stay at home until you've finished your business then get the hell out. I can even put an officer on your door providing you make every effort to sell and move.'

Martin thanked the sergeant for his understanding and kindness, and as they drove back he began to wonder where he should go next. With the house sold he'd be set to make quite a profit.

The police radio crackled and a voice came through the speaker.

We have a potential problem in Queen Street, it informed them through the static.

'That's my street,' Martin became alarmed.

A mob has gathered. They seem to be congregating at number sixteen.

Jack picked up the radio and spoke into it, 'That's Martin Powell's house. I'm heading over now.'

You might want back up, it's getting rowdy.

Queen Street swelled with angry residents. The article in today's paper had been incendiary enough to whip up a hate mob hell bent on driving the convicted sex attacker from his home. They jeered and shouted at number sixteen, shouting insults and booing at the empty windows. They threw stones against the glass, trying to bait the resident to show himself, not knowing that he was not there.

Damage has been reported, the radio informed.

The mob drew closer to the property and grew braver with their protest. Someone took a spray paint canister and wrote the word *SCUM* in large red letters across the front door.

The sirens wailed and the lights flashed as Martin and Sergeant Jack sped to his home. A home under attack.

The crowd egged each other on, becoming more violent and daring as their choice of missile changed from stones to bricks to bottles. The urban artillery flew through the air and smashed into the windows, breaking the panes and sending the sharp fragments scattering through the house. Inside the sieged home there was no one but the puppets to witness the onslaught of public disgust.

Mr Starr was glad he'd delayed setting off on his holiday for a few hours, despite lying to his daughter Pippa. As he lit a rag that hung out the end of a bottle he smiled. All these years he'd waited for his revenge. The flame illuminated a vengeful delight on his face as he tossed the Molotov cocktail in through a broken window. The bottle smashed on the living room floor, spilling its petrol contents that immediately ignited from the burning rag. The flames spread quickly throughout the house engulfing every room, one by one. The destructive, orange glow flickered from the windows and the mob cheered with malicious joy.

As the police car arrived on the scene the crowd bolted in all directions to escape arrest, alerted by the flashing lights and siren. Within a few moments the only two left to witness the house burn were Sergeant Jack and a distraught Martin. The blaze cast the silhouette of a sorrowful man as he fell to his knees and watched his life and memories disintegrate in front of him. Even his tears were taken as they evaporated against the heat of the inferno.

14

J. R. Park

Martin sat in the charred carcass of a building he once called home. The walls were black from the fire and sodden from the water hoses.

The fire brigade had only taken minutes to arrive and it wasn't long before the blaze had been extinguished. The fire chief had explained that the house was structurally sound but this was little comfort to Martin. It wasn't the walls or foundations that he cherished. He sat on the floor of the living room and opened a badly burnt, wooden box he had retrieved from the wardrobe. Its edges had been burnt away, rounding them and darkening the wood so it looked more like an old fashioned chest. He gently sobbed as he anticipated the damage inside.

Sergeant Jack had taken pity on the distraught puppeteer. He had explained that this was a crime scene and there were proper procedures to follow, but Martin begged him to be let inside and try to retrieve some important mementos that he held dear. Confronted with such a heartfelt plea from such a tragic victim Jack acquiesced and allowed him one hour; there would be an officer on the door for his safety.

He opened the lid to the wooden box, the charcoal crumbling in his hands as he pulled it apart. Inside was a photo album. He groaned as he saw what he had feared, the fire had burnt the edges of the album and the heat had blistered the photographs on each page. Martin flicked through the pages and looked at images, washed of colour and barely recognisable. They were images of older times, happier times, before he went to prison. He stopped on one and studied it. He could make out his own smile and next to him in the photo there was a wave of auburn hair, but the rest was warped and burnt beyond recognition.

Tears trickled down his cheeks as he fingered the burnt lines of the picture.

They took my life, he thought, my happy life. They took my life and now they've taken my memories.

Through all the horrors he endured in prison he always knew they would come to an end. He knew he would be released and that he could start his life over. With every humiliation he suffered he would cast his mind back to his most happy memories, building a mental wall with which to protect himself. The thought of being able to get some of that life back when his sentence was complete fortified those barriers.

With a destroyed album in his hands he sat alone and in the darkness. His links to the past were gone, his hopes for the future in tatters. How much more abuse would he suffer? Could he escape the past if he moved? It only took one rumour, one newspaper story and it would all start up again. Was there any escape? As these thoughts looped in his brain he felt despair grip his very soul. His hope had vanished, his defences were down, his mental walls had crumbled.

Ha ha ha ha ha ha.

What was that? Martin thought.

Was he dreaming? The last time he heard that sound he'd been asleep, but this was no revery now. Where was it coming from? As he got to his feet he picked up the bat. He was pleased that, at least, had survived the fire.

'You're no rat,' he called out, 'who the hell is there?'

Inching toward the sound of laughter he found the source to be coming from behind the remains of the sofa. He crept round the mess of badly burnt furnishings to discover a blanket. It had caught the fire but mostly suffered smoke and water damage. Crumpled underneath a nest of tables it had acquired some protection and escaped the worst of the blaze. He turned his ear to the scrunched up rag; the laughing seemed to be coming from under the blanket! Slowly Martin reached out and with a swift tug pulled it to reveal what was hiding underneath.

Instantly the laughing ceased as the blanket came away revealing the Mr Punch costume. The grotesque mask had warped and bent in the heat of the fire making it look twisted and malformed. Its smile seemed to look more threatening and its eyes appeared to widen with a sinister gaze.

Martin's look of shock upon viewing the

survivor soon gave way to laughter. At first it was nothing more than a gentle chuckle of relief but the more he regarded the fire tainted figure in front of him the more he laughed. His mirth grew manic until it sounded like the noises heard in his dreams.

'You haven't left me,' he bellowed between guffaws.

He took his bat and swung it round, smashing it against the remains of the sofa. Laughing as the wooden bat crashed down, it sent pieces of charcoal and ash scattering everywhere.

'Stupid town,' he cried.

He swung his bat again, striking against a shelf and pulling it from its fittings. He whooped with delight as it fell to the floor.

'You took my life!' he shouted.

Without looking he swung the bat around, almost turning himself three hundred and sixty degrees, so violent was the action. The bat landed squarely on his television, cracking the screen and knocking it to the floor.

As the destruction grew greater, his laugh grew more manic and his rants louder.

'You took my lover!' he shouted.

He swung at the coffee table, one of its legs giving out on the impact and collapsing to the floor.

'My dignity!'

The bookcase fell forward from the next hit, slumping to the ground and spilling its contents.

'My joy!'

Again and again Martin lashed out at the objects in the room. He didn't even look to aim knowing that the bat would eventually come into contact with something and continue to satisfy his destructive desire. The clock, the dinner plates, the dining table, the corner lamp, the lights, all smashed to pieces as he swung and hit and destroyed.

'It's time I took some revenge,' he paused, out of breath from his moment of mayhem.

In the debris that littered the floor Martin caught sight of his swazzle. Picking it up he placed it in his mouth and began to speak through the device. The fire had caused the small contraption some damage, making the sound it produced lower and rougher to the ear.

'You're going to get it,' he spoke with the fire affected effect. 'You are all going to get it. I'll make them pay!' He swung his bat again, 'Make them pay! Make them pay!'

'Hello? Mr Powell, are you okay?'

Police Constable Williams had been ordered to wait outside of number sixteen, give the man an hour then bring him to the station. It had only been a little over thirty minutes but the policeman had heard something going on inside the house. Had someone snuck in and decided to take their revenge personally, away from the mob? As much as he disliked Powell this was not going to happen on his watch.

'Hello?' he called out again to the silence of the house.

He walked into what was left of the sitting room. This is more than fire damage, thought Williams as he nervously stepped through the mess. Fragments of broken furniture and ornaments were strewn across the floor. He stumbled as he walked, his foot catching on the household rubble. The room was dark in the evening light with no electricity to illuminate the soot covered surroundings, making it difficult to see where he was placing his feet.

Suddenly he felt something hit him across the face. Something hard. The impact knocked him off his balance and sent him crashing to the floor. He felt blood trickle from his temple as the fresh wound throbbed. Laughter came from somewhere in the room but the darkness concealed his attacker.

Quickly PC Williams scrabbled to his feet and called out, 'Who's there?'

Again, from the darkness, the policeman was struck, this time to the stomach. He felt the air being forced out of his lungs as he dropped to his knees, desperate for breath. This time when he looked up, the twilight gave up his aggressor. Through the gloom a freakish face appeared only a few feet from his. Underneath a tall, elf-like hat appeared eyes, wild and frenzied. Its twisted nose came down in a hook and framed, with its long pointed chin, a wide, evil, fixed grin.

The figure held a large wooden bat with both hands and raised the weapon above its head.

'Oh hell,' muttered PC Williams.

'Oh hell indeed,' screamed Punch, his voice like sandpaper on a blackboard.

Punch brought the bat down hard on Williams's cranium. The force caused his head to split open and knocked him onto his back. Blood gushed from the injury. He held his hand up to stop the next strike, but the bat caught his fingers and he heard them snap as they bent backwards. He howled in pain but was silenced with the next swing. It caught the side of his jaw, knocking three teeth to the floor in a pool of blood. His head slammed hard against the ground and his eyes rolled in their sockets. The crazed lunatic showed no mercy as, strike after strike, he battered the defenceless officer with relentless fury; laughing with each horrific crack of bone and spray of blood.

'You're going to get it,' cried Punch. 'You're all going to get it. Mr Punch is going to get them!'

J. R. Park

15

J. R. Park

As the crowd gathered in the town centre the pier remained quiet. All staff had finished for the day and now lined the high street, ready for the festivities that lay ahead. The arcade machines continued to flash and bleep their endless patterns, illuminating the dimly lit pier as the night drew in. Only an automated change converter stood by to assist any potential customers that might happen to wander this way, bored of the procession of floats and marching bands that were poised to make their way through the town centre.

Pete, Jordan and Paul sat outside on a pier bench, their vodka saturated bloodstreams protecting them from the coastal breeze.

'So what's the plan for later?' Paul asked before taking a large drag on a spliff. 'Are we heading down to the carnival tonight?'

'Hell yeah,' replied Jordan taking the spliff from

his friend's fingers.

'But we haven't got any costumes,' Pete noted as he looked longingly at the red cherry glow of the herbal cigarette.

'Do I look like I'm going to wear a fucking costume?' Jordan pulled a face at this idea as he blew out a large puff of white smoke. 'Fancy dress is for freaks and losers.'

'Still, all the chicks will be out,' Paul nudged Jordan and took back the spliff.

'That's for sure. I hear Pippa is going in burlesque. Hot!' Pete toasted his thought with a swig of neat vodka, straight from the bottle.

'Back off man,' Jordan leant forward and swiped the bottle from his hands, 'I got dibs on her.'

He gulped a mouthful of vodka. The alcohol burnt the back of his throat and made him cough. He pulled a disgusted face and spluttered, 'That's some nasty shit!'

'Give me some,' Paul demanded, desperate to keep his buzz going.

Their conversation was interrupted by an unusual sound. It sounded like something solid and hard being dragged along the ground. As the sound got louder and more distinct they knew something was getting closer.

'What the fuck?' Paul put the bottle to the ground and stood up, unsure of what he was looking at.

In the shadows they could see the silhouette of a person walking towards them. It held a long pole or rod whose end was being run along the ground producing the teeth clenching scraping noise as the figure drew closer. The flashes from the arcade machines shone through the windows of the amusement hut and danced on the features of the approaching stranger, offering glimpses of his appearance. But it was only when he got a few feet away from the three young man that they could clearly make him out.

'Uggggh,' said Pete, 'that is ugly.'

The twisted features of the grotesque mask grinned with psychotic mania as Punch drew closer, all the while dragging his bat on the ground.

'You know what you were saying about freaks and losers?' Pete said to Jordan, keeping his eyes focused on the costumed man that approached.

'Looks like we have a Class A one right here!' Jordan said.

Punch stood in front of the gang of three, his presence made more eerie by his silence.

'Are you lost?' Pete asked, unsure what to do.

Punch continued to keep his silence. He regarded the men for a few moments before swiping his bat at the vodka by Paul's feet. The bottle shattered into pieces whilst the vodka soaked into Paul's shoes. The men were stunned momentarily at the sudden and unprovoked violence.

'Oh I see,' Jordan challenged, 'you want to play do you? You want to-'

Before he could finish the sentence Punch swung the bat and hit the gang leader full in the face. He fell back against a wall, clutching his nose whilst blood poured from the gaps between his fingers. In quick succession three more blows were delivered. His nose disintegrated with a crimson explosion on the first strike.

The second and third hit his skull so hard his eyes were pushed back into their sockets and the bat needed to be wiggled free from the huge split across his head. In less than a minute Jordan had been beaten to death.

Pete took a knife from his pocket and dived at the costumed murderer. Punch swung at him and knocked the man and his knife into the arcade room. Pete tried to keep his balance but stumbled and tripped onto a pinball machine, his face crashing down onto the glass top covering. Quickly Punch ran to where he lay, spread over the amusement machine, and battered him with his weapon. The ferocious poundings drove Pete's beaten and misshapen head through the glass, as broken shards sliced his neck, severing arteries and spraying blood in every direction.

Paul ran inside to help his friend, but upon seeing his fate reconsidered and turned round to flee. Seeing Punch clock him he dived to the floor and hid within the aisles of arcade machines. Paul crawled on the floor to find safety as he heard the attackers bat scrape along ground.

'Where are you?' Punch taunted as he walked up and down the aisle. 'Mr Punch is going to teach you some manners.'

Paul reached into his pocket and pulled out a lock blade penknife. He opened up the six inch blade and locked it into position. The feel of the weapon in his hand brought him renewed courage as he crawled to the end of the aisle. The sound of the bat scraping on the ground was getting closer.

'Mr Punch wants to see you,' Punch called out.

The voice was close, Paul sensed the maniac

was only a few feet away; just the other side of the machine he was using for cover. Taking a few deep breaths and gripping the knife tightly he pounced round the corner, rising to his feet to take on this murderous abomination. His bravery was unfounded however as the aisle was empty. Paul looked around in panic as Punch's crazed voice floated around the room.

'That's right. Come find me.'

Where was the bastard, thought Paul as his eyes darted around the room.

The sound of the bat scraping on the floor seemed to come from everywhere. He ducked down and caught sight of the bright costumed tights the lunatic wore in the gaps between the arcade machines. Paul stayed low and lightly ran to the end of the next aisle waiting for Punch to get closer. He counted to five and then dived round the corner.

Again it was empty!

The room fell silent.

Where was he hiding?

Was this just some kind of crazy nightmare?

The scraping sound had stopped and the gentle lapping of the waves below was the only thing he could hear. He called out and waited for a moment, his knife poised for an attack, but no one replied. Mystified, Paul turned to leave the seemingly empty building. As he turned he came face to face with the goggle eyed mask. The fixed grin seemed to grow wider as Punch swung the bat, delivering a heavy blow.

'That's the way to do it!' Punch screeched as he rained devastating blows of wild aggression onto the early twenty something. As his cheekbone split and his forearm snapped in two he let out chilling screams of a man that knew he was going to die. His cries rolled across a deserted pier and were swallowed up by the sea. No one was around to hear the beginning of the end for Stanswick Sands.

16

Colin studied the pier through the window of the Minstrel café, oblivious to the scenes of slaughter that were happening over the road. Had the music not been blasting out the speakers in the deserted café he might have caught the screams of three men meeting their perilous ends. The café was due to close and he had stopped by to pick up his girlfriend Jo, ready for the carnival. He chewed on some sausages that Jo had lovingly prepared, awaiting his arrival, and he swung on a stool whilst dressed in a crocodile outfit. The green and yellow suit had a soft tail that dragged on the floor as he span.

'These sure are tasty, Jo,' Colin said as he stopped the spinning stool to face her, his elbows resting on the counter.

'The best for you honey,' she smiled, 'even if you are wearing the dumbest outfit.'

'Aww come on,' he looked down at himself for a moment, 'it's a laugh. It's almost closing time, do you want to get your costume on?'

'Yeah okay,' she replied with a loving look. 'Can you watch the diner whilst I nip out back and get changed?'

'No problems honey.'

Colin had helped shut the café down many times, especially on a Saturday night. But tonight he had more of a reason to be here than just to get out and enjoy the festivities early.

'Thanks sexy,' Jo looked into her lover's eyes, 'and thanks for showing up. I've been so worried since I saw Mr Powell come in here the other day.'

'You needn't worry baby,' he puffed out his chest, 'I showed him a thing or two. He won't be bothering you again.'

Jo blew him a kiss and gleefully skipped into a back room to get changed. Colin watched the back room door close and could make out the shape of his beautiful girlfriend through the frosted glass as she began to take her clothes off.

He was glad Martin Powell had walked into the pub this afternoon whilst he had been there. Admittedly he was as shocked as everyone else to have seen him, but for the honour of his lover he made sure he was the first person to take a stand and punch the sick bastard to the ground.

'Can you turn the music and lights off please babe?' Jo shouted through the door.

She bopped to the sound of music pumping through a pair of headphones as she slid chequered lycra leggings from her harlequin costume over her smooth, shapely thighs.

He leant over the counter and switched the music off then, with the last song playing still in his head and an air of satisfaction in his movements, Colin half danced across the café and flicked the light switches, plunging the dining area into near darkness. As he headed back to his seat to finish his sausage supper he felt a gust of cold wind and the bell above the entrance jingled.

'Sorry pal we're closing up,' he said with his back still to the door.

Turning round he saw a man dressed as Mr Punch stood in the doorway. Even through the darkness Colin could make out the fire damage to the costume that twisted its features.

'Wow,' he said, startled by the appearance of the stranger, 'that costume has seen better days.'

Punch softly patted his bat into his hand for a moment, not saying a word. They both looked at each other for a short while before the crazed character broke the stand off and walked towards Colin.

'Hey buddy,' the man in the crocodile outfit called out, 'didn't you hear me? I said we were closing.'

Ignoring Colin's words Punch carried on across the café, bashing tables and chairs out of his way as he continued on his path to revenge. The furniture smashed into pieces as it crashed against the walls and disintegrated under the force of his bat.

'What the fuck?'

Colin was taken aback by this sudden act of violence but he was not the kind of guy to run from a threat. He picked up a chair and threw it at the approaching maniac. The chair broke into three as

Punch batted it away before it could hit him. Grabbing the stool he had been sat on, Colin lifted it above his head and hurled it. Again Punch swatted it from the air.

'Motherfucker,' Colin looked around for something more substantial he could use as weapon.

Taking hold of a table in front of him, Colin lifted it into the air, but before he had chance to project his new piece of artillery Punch came charging at him. With a swing from his bat he hit Colin in the stomach. Winded, he dropped the table as he stumbled backwards. A kick to the legs brought Colin crashing down on the counter. Dazed and injured he lay, slumped over the counter, helpless as Punch approached him.

Taking his time, Punch lined his bat up against the man's head as it hung over the counter edge. Raising the bat high above him he paused, savouring the moment, before smashing it down on Colin's skull.

Jo had almost finished getting changed in the backroom. She had taken a while to sort out the frills around her neck and to get her hair tied up and neatly tucked away under the headpiece. The headpiece had two bells; each one hung off a point and jingled as she moved. Jo had worried the sound may annoy her later in the night but at that moment she couldn't hear anything over the music coming through her headphones. She applied the finishing touches to her black and white face paints oblivious to the silhouette of Punch through the frosted glass behind her. The silhouette swung its bat again and again, with each swing more blood sprayed against the window.

'Don't forget the bolt,' she called out to her

boyfriend in a voice unsure of its own volume.

She waited a moment for a reply. Taking her headphones out of her ears Jo listened again but the café was silent.

'Hun? Colin?' Jo called out. 'Can you make sure the bolt is down.'

Still not hearing anything Jo inquisitively walked through the door and back out into the dining area. The sight that met her was so horrific it took the screams from her throat. Illuminated by the light from the back room like some cruel spotlight, her boyfriend's body lay, slumped over the counter, his neck ending in a mess of ragged, torn flesh and protruding bone as the splintered spinal column jutted out at an awkward angle. The room was soaked in blood from floor to ceiling and his headless corpse still twitched in a pool of its own scarlet fluids.

Terrified, Jo began to whimper when all of sudden the back room light went out leaving the café in total darkness. Collecting her wits she made a dash to the exit. She turned the handle and pulled at the door but it would not budge. The door was locked!

She turned to face the café again; frightened that someone might be creeping up behind her in the darkness. She strained her eyes but couldn't see anything in the inky blackness. Outside two police cars pulled up by the pier, their flashing lights began to wash the café in a strobing, blue light. Jo watched four policemen emerge from their vehicles and head towards the amusement arcade. She called out and banged on the glass, desperate to draw their attention, but they couldn't hear her through the double glazed windows. What Jo needed was something to break the glass. As she turned back to the carnage in the café, to find something heavy enough to use, she froze. Standing in front of her was Punch, flickering in and out of vision with the flashing of the police lights. Slowly he began to circle her like a hungry wolf, his image captured in the strobe effect like lights on the spokes of a wheel.

'What do you want?' Jo screamed out hysterically.

'Do you not recognise me?' Punch asked. 'You recognised me the other day didn't you? I have one of those faces.'

'Oh my god,' Jo remembered their exchange and realised who was lurking behind that deformed mask, 'Martin Powell?'

'You destroyed Martin Powell years ago,' he spoke with vehement disgust. 'You and your friend destroyed that poor man with your lies.'

'We didn't mean to,' she cried with genuine regret.

'Evil!' Punch shouted before diving towards her.

He swung his bat at her legs and knocked her to the floor. Jo collapsed in pain and screamed as she held her thigh. Already she could feel the bruised area throb. The young girl climbed back on to her unsteady feet, but as soon as she did so he swung his bat again. It struck the same thigh, and with a powerful blow sent her crashing to the ground. Not waiting for her to get up this time he took another swipe, hitting her ankle with a loud crack. Jo howled in pain as her foot bent round, forming a right angle with her leg. She clutched at her ankle, knowing it was broken.

'It wasn't me,' she begged, 'it wasn't me!'

Jo struggled to her feet, but as she tried to stand her legs gave out and she fell to the floor. She tried again but collapsed in an agonizing scream. Unable to stand she began to crawl to the window.

There must be a way of signaling to the officers outside.

Punch watched the pathetic scene as Jo pulled herself across the bloodied floor with her arms and banged on the window. The glass was too thick to let out any sound and her cries for help went unheard. The police had their attention focused in the opposite direction, but even if they did turnaround and look towards her the café was so dark that there would be little to make out from so far away.

Punch walked over to the girl and stood above her, straddling Jo as she lay on the floor crying at the window.

'It wasn't me,' she cried, 'it was all Pippa's idea.'

'I'm sure it was,' Punch was not impressed.

'It was...It was!' Jo begged him.

'And where's Pippa?' he asked. 'Where?'

'Twelve Quick Lane,' Jo found herself saying in desperation to stave off the attack. 'Please-'

Punch felt no sympathy or remorse as he drove the bat down into her head. With a gleeful frenzy that had been building for a decade he bludgeoned her skull until it cracked and brain matter spilled into the headpiece of her costume. The pink, jelly-like substance oozed from the wounds as her lifeless hand ran down the glass, her potential saviours only metres away.

17

'Hey baby, I'm sorry.'

Chloe was perched on the kitchen work surface with a phone against her ear. She was a petite girl with a homely charm. She played with her ginger hair, curling it around her fingers whilst she talked to her boyfriend. She had been a little disappointed not to be heading out to the carnival this year but when Pippa called and offered her a premium rate to baby sit it was an offer she couldn't turn down.

'Sorry you can't come over,' she said to her boyfriend, Jim, who was growing horny on the other end of the phone. 'If she finds out you came over tonight she'll freak. We'll have to wait for another time.'

Chloe laid back on the kitchen counter and began to rub her crotch, stimulating her clitoris through the fabric of her jeans. She smiled a dirty smile as she listened to Jim talk suggestively with breathy tones.

'Hey listen,' she said, 'if I'm a good girl tonight, look after the baby and behave myself then maybe I'll be able to have that party next week, and then I can be a bad girl.'

She giggled as she listened to the response of her lustful boyfriend.

Police sirens screamed down the street and past the house causing Chloe to sit up with a start.

'Wow it must be a wild night in town,' she remarked.

A bang echoed round the house as the back door swung open and slammed against the inside wall. It startled Chloe for a moment until she worked out what it was.

'Stupid dog,' she sighed. 'Sorry Jim, the damn dog has pushed the door open again. Give me a few minutes, I'll call you back later.'

Chloe blew kisses down the phone then hung up.

'Stupid dog,' she muttered again as she slid off the counter. 'Toby, wait until I get hold of you. Toby!' Chloe called out.

On command a black Labrador came bounding down the stairs.

'Toby!' Chloe looked confused, 'If you've been upstairs then...?'

Her voice trailed off as she nervously pointed to the back door that swung back and forth by the evening wind. Her dismissive attitude was suddenly taken over by a sense of fear. No one else should be here and she was certain she closed the door earlier. She picked up the phone from the side and cautiously the teenager approached the door. She looked out into the night, the wind howled in her face and thunder gently rumbled in the distance. The back garden, however, was empty. With a sense of relief Chloe slammed the door shut, this time taking care to turn the lock.

Toby had been stood where he was called, watching the babysitter lock the door when all of a sudden he began to bark wildly and growl. His large canines where shown in a display of aggression as he stared, focused on the door.

Bang! Bang! Bang!

The door shook and rattled as someone started hammering it from the other side. Out of fright Chloe jumped, dropping the phone, and ran behind the Labrador for protection.

Bang! Bang! Bang!

The sounds grew in volume as the blows increased with power. The door shook in its frame and threatened to burst from its hinges.

Bang! Bang! Bang!

Cracks began to appear down the body of the door and the screws chimed as they bounced off the tiled floor. Chloe crouched to her knees and held her head in her hands. She began to panic as the door showed signs of yielding to the attacker. Any rational thought had been replaced by terror as she let out an ear splitting scream.

All of a sudden the banging ceased. Toby stopped barking. Everything was still.

Chloe needed to get help. Running out the front door was an option, but what if the attacker was there waiting for her? Her best option was to call someone. The police? Jim? It didn't matter. The phone lay at the foot of the back door where she had dropped it in fright.

Unsure if the attacker might still be out there she edged, inch by inch, to the damaged frame, daring not to breathe as if the door itself would notice her and come to life. Keeping as far away as she could Chloe stretched out her hand then, with a fast motion, grabbed the receiver.

A doorbell rang and gave her a start.

She realised it was the front door. Was it the attacker or a friend? Running to the front door Chloe placed her eye to the spy hole and looked through. She smiled with relief to see a friendly face the other side. Unbolting the door in a hurry she raced to let her rescuer in.

'Oh Colin it's so good to see-'

Chloe lost the words to finish her sentence. As she opened the door she saw Punch stood in front of her holding Colin's decapitated head by the hair. Blood still dribbled from the crudely severed neck. The babysitter walked backwards, falling over her own feet, and landed heavily on the floor. Within an instant Toby launched himself at the costumed killer, but before he could land an attack he was knocked to the floor, hit in mid air by Punch's bat. Toby had no time to get to his paws as Punch immediately set on him. Chloe watched, transfixed in horror, as Punch pulverized the poor animal to a bloody paste.

'Well, well if it isn't Pippa,' he turned to the girl. 'You ruined my life.'

'I'm not Pippa,' Chloe protested.

'Lies! I'd thought you'd have grown out of them by now,' he screamed as he swung his bat, his mind confused and clouded by bloodlust.

Chloe dodged his weapon as it just missed her and crashed onto the kitchen surface. Her pathway to the front door was blocked but if she could get through the already broken back door she could escape. Sprinting on her heels she ran to the back of the house. Punch gave chase and caught her ankle with his bat. She tripped and fell into the conservatory, crashing into shelves lined with tools and spilling their contents to the floor. Picking up a handful of nails that had fallen out of a box she threw them at Punch. They bounced off him with little effect.

'You've hurt me once already,' he taunted, 'you couldn't possibly do me any more damage you little bitch!'

The phone began to ring in the kitchen. Chloe looked across to the receiver, she was cornered in the conservatory and the only way to it was through Punch. He swung at the young girl and struck her, knocking her to the floor.

'No one can save you now,' he roared.

He stood above the defenceless babysitter as blood streamed from a cut across her forehead. She was conscious but dazed. He raised his bat above his head ready to take his revenge when the answerphone started up, playing the message on loudspeaker.

'Hi it's Pippa,' the speaker buzzed with the message being left.

Punch turned his ear and listened to the call.

'Hope you're okay,' it continued, 'the carnival is going great. The burlesque idea was brilliant. The judges seem to be really going for it and we are set to win. The procession is about to head off round the streets so I have to go. It's raining but I'll be okay.'

His mind began to clear and slowly it sank in to Punch that he had the wrong person. This wasn't Pippa! This wasn't who he'd bumped into in the supermarket! Enraged he turned back to the girl only to find she had gone. She must have taken the opportunity whilst he'd been distracted and run off. Where moments before lay a ginger haired girl, all that was there now was a small pool of blood and a floor strewn with nails. He prodded the nails idly with his bat whilst he formulated his next plan. It was time to go to the carnival.

18

Today was a nightmare before Sergeant Jack had even stepped foot onto the horrific crime scene in the Minstrel café. The carnival was always going to stretch the town's limited police force, but the minor riot that ended in the burning down of Martin Powell's house had put them over their resource threshold. Overtime and Specials were going to be called for. And it was whilst he was worrying about this that the report came through: three bodies had been found, murdered on the pier. Not just murdered, but bludgeoned, taken apart. Nothing like this had happened in Stanswick Sands and it needed his utmost attention. Whilst driving to the sea front to speak with the investigating team already there another call came through, two more bodies had been discovered in the Minstrel café, opposite the aging pier. As he stepped through the crime scene tape and into the café, still splattered floor to ceiling with blood, he realised it was actually only one and a half bodies. This fact made his stomach twitch as he felt some bile rise to the back of his throat.

'What the fuck is this?' Jack pointed at a black and white image on a TV screen.

The CCTV had captured scenes of Punch in the café whilst on his murderous rampage. The footage had been paused on the clearest image of the figure as he stood in the dining area, weapon in hand. The viewing screen was small and the picture grainy but his wild grin and hooked nose were clear to see.

'It's Mr Punch, sir,' came the reply from Constable Rawlings.

'I can see it's Mr Punch!' The sergeant began to pace, 'What the fuck is going on? We have dead bodies all over the place and now it seems some maniac in a Punch outfit is running around clubbing people to death.'

'Sorry to interrupt,' Constable Knew apologised with an ashen colour face, a look filled with dread, 'we've just had a report from PC Comer, she went up to Martin Powell's house to check on Williams. She found Williams in the house. He's dead. Beaten to death.'

'Oh God,' Jack shook his head, this night was getting worse by the minute, 'has anyone contacted Williams's family?'

'Control are on it,' Knew replied.

'And what of Powell?' Jack's voice sounded weary, unsure if he wanted to know the answer.

'No sign of him,' Knew answered.

'Do we have any IDs on these victims?' Jack turned to Rawlings.

'We still haven't found this guy's head,' Rawlings pointed to the decapitated corpse, 'but according to his wallet this is Colin Kiln. And that over there is his girlfriend a Miss Joanna King.'

'Wasn't the King girl involved in the Powell case?' Knew asked.

'She was one of the victims he abused when she was a little girl,' PC Rawlings replied, 'poor lass.'

'And those lads at the pier,' Jack asked them both, 'any connection to the Powell case?'

'Not really,' came Rawlings reply.

'Not really?' Jack sounded astonished by the uncertainty in his answer.

'Well no connection to the case,' Knew piped up, adding clarity, 'but they were the ones that gave him a right good kicking outside the George this afternoon.'

'Really,' Jack's forehead began to crease with worry, 'and this girl wasn't the only one involved in the case. There was another, a Pippa Starr.'

'That's correct,' PC Knew nodded.

'And where is Starr now?'

Rawlings spoke like it was obvious, 'She'll be at the carnival. She's on one of the floats tonight. A head turning burlesque theme and looking pretty fine.'

As he finished his sentence his tone lightened and the two constables sniggered briefly to one another. The inappropriate and crude mood was missed by their boss as he pondered for a moment. The pieces were fitting together and as wild as the theory was that brewed in Sergeant Jack's mind, it was the best they had.

'You don't think she's in trouble do you, sir?' PC Rawlings saw the grave expression on his face.

'I can't say for certain, but Powell is missing and the King girl is dead. If it is Powell and he is seeking revenge then sure as hell Pippa Starr will be the next target. Radio ahead, we need to get to the carnival, find Pippa and find that damn maniac!'

19

The turnout for the carnival even surpassed the enthusiastic and optimistic visions of its organisers. The town square and high street were full of revelers and each one had made an effort to dress up. Amongst the pirates, super heroes and whatever else the residents and visitors had decided to come as, circus performers engaged in acts of skillful entertainment from plate spinning to fire breathing to close up magic tricks. The crowd whooped with joy and ignored the light drizzle of rain that had begun to sprinkle on their celebrations. Kaspar was dressed as a clown whilst his mum, Grete, had come as a slinky, black cat complete with a velvet tail and painted on whiskers. Kaspar watched in awe as fireworks lit up the night sky. This was the signal that the procession of floats and marching bands were to make their way through the streets.

The police hurriedly moved through the crowd. The sea of costumed revelers made it a difficult task to search for the man dressed in the Punch costume. Here and there they caught hold of people thinking they might have spotted the insane killer but each time it turned out to be a clown or a jester. Each costume was not quite the same as the twisted evil they had been shown from the CCTV footage.

As the marching bands played and the majorettes stepped to the beat, twirling their batons, the floats burst into life with a garish mixture of bright lights and loud music. Pippa and her friends danced on a trailer that been decorated with flashing disco lights, glitter and pink feathers. The heat from the coloured bulbs kept the cold at bay as they performed their planned routines wearing lacy basques, feather boas, fish net stockings and stiletto heels.

'Police seem to be a bit rough down there tonight,' Sally said to Pippa as they looked down at the crowd that had lined the streets.

They watched the officers pushing their way through and questioning people with increasing force and desperation.

'Yeah, what the hell's going on?' Pippa wondered with concerned curiosity.

The bat dragged along the ground, but this time it screeched and grinded like the sound of a broken dentist's drill. Nails had been crudely driven into the end of the wooden weapon; they jutted out at all manner of angles and scratched at the ground as its carrier walked through the deserted backstreets.

'There!' shouted Sergeant Jack as he pointed at Pippa. 'I want a group of officers following that float.'

Four constables and specials squeezed through the spectators and took up position, two either side of the float, and walked alongside it. Their eyes were trained on the crowd, looking out for the crazed and maniacal Punch.

The nails ripped white trails into the stone as their sharp ends were pulled across the paving slabs. Blood slowly dripped down the shaft of the weapon and Punch's knuckles grew white under his gloves as he clenched the bat tight with vengeful hate.

'We have the girl secured sir,' PC Andrews radioed to Jack as he kept his watch by the side of the decorated trailer, 'no sign of Powell or the costume.'

'Good, stay with her,' Jack radioed back.

The sergeant stayed within the throng of the crowd, glancing at every window, every alleyway, every person over five and a half feet tall in fancy dress. Punch could be anywhere, anyone, hiding in plain sight!

'I can't see a thing in this crowd,' Jack radioed through to his team by the float.

'Don't worry sir,' Andrews called back with confidence, 'if he's here he's not getting past us.'

The dustbins bent and folded as easy as kitchen foil as an enraged Punch smashed his bat into them. The extra strength of the nails in the end adding both weight and force to the murderous weapon he carried.

The procession was reaching halfway although there was a slight bottleneck going through the old town gates.

They weren't designed for large trailers to travel through and so the drivers had to take it slow. The sides of the floats were barely a foot away from the edge as they made it under the archway. This allowed Sergeant Jack and his men more time to check the crowd on the other side before Pippa and her float were to pass through. At last something was going in their favour.

Grete danced with Kaspar to the music of the marching band and then glanced at her watch.

'Come on Kaspar,' she said, 'I have a surprise for you.'

The two walked out of the crowd, hand in hand and towards the pier.

The George was as crowded as the streets outside. The alcohol flowed freely as did the money, which made Greg smile. He always had his regulars but it was nights like tonight that really kept his business afloat. Even the most hardened of locals had made an effort for the carnival and had come in fancy dress. It wasn't really Greg's sort of thing, he felt a bit past it at fifty-two, but to show willing he wore an eye patch and made the sound of a pirate when taking orders. This seemed to raise a few smiles amongst the busy crush at the bar.

'Judith,' Greg called to his barmaid, 'can you look after the bar for a moment, I'm just popping out back to change a barrel.'

Judith smiled and dutifully held the fort whilst the barman headed out towards the back of the pub. He stepped outside into the alleyway behind the George and put a cigarette in his mouth. The air was a little cold and a fine mist of rain was coming down, but neither of these things bothered him. On the contrary they seemed to refresh him from his evening's work. Greg lit the cigarette and took a few steps into the alley. The security light flicked on revealing his bins to have been knocked over, rubbish was strewn everywhere.

'Bloody seagulls,' he muttered as he set to work righting the fallen bins.

A noise echoed down the alleyway. Unsure of what it was Greg looked through the shadows but could see no one.

'Hello?' he called out. 'Anyone there?'

He waited a few moments before cursing the seagulls once more.

The noise grew louder, a vile, scraping sound that pricked his ears; the aural equivalent of splinters under your fingernails. Greg gritted his teeth as the noise intensified. At first all he could make out was an evil grin that seemed to glow in the dark, but slowly the stranger became clearer. Punch emerged from the night, scratching his bat along the ground. The halogen security light illuminated Punch, detailing every burn and blood stain in minute glory.

The cigarette fell from Greg's startled, open mouth, but before he could react Punch swung his bat. It hit the barman on the back of the head; the nails that had been so crudely driven in punctured his skull and stuck fast. Punch pulled the bat backwards and brought Greg's convulsing body crashing into the dustbins. He still remained attached to the bat, which was swung viciously against the wooden fence next to them. Again and again Punch launched the bat at the fence, driving

Greg's face into the panels. His nose splintered into fragments and his teeth were smashed out of their gums.

'Thank you for my lovely pint of beer this afternoon,' Punch mocked the dead man as he continued his onslaught. 'I'll make sure to come again!'

A red circle of gore grew wider on the fence with each impact like a twisted Rorschach diagram as his forehead cracked and his face was reduced to a crumbled mess of blood so thick it looked black. Punch placed his foot on top of the corpses head and slowly levered the bat from his skull. The crunch of bone filled the alley as the nails were prised away, pieces of hair and brain still clinging to the end of his horrific weapon.

'Please sir.'

The voice gave Punch a start as he turned round, ready to attack. From out of the shadows stepped an old man with long, grey, unwashed hair. His clothes were dirty and stained with grime. He wore sunglasses and held a white cane in his left hand that gently waved through the air as he shuffled towards the dead man and his killer.

'Can you spare a bit of a change for a poor, blind man?'

Punch lowered his bat and silently regarded the sightless hobo.

The police kept their watch on the crowd, but as Pippa's float traveled through the archway of the old town gates those that followed the float had to abandon their posts and walk round the other side. It was just too narrow to walk alongside. It was whilst the four officers were walking round that they heard a scream come from the other end. Racing round they found the body of Patrick Taylor, he was the local tramp and blind. His lifeless body lay on the road under the wheels of a tractor that had been pulling one of the floats, his long, grey hair stained red with blood.

'What happened?' asked PC Andrews to a shocked crowd.

Punch stood on top of the archway and watched the mayhem below. His plan of throwing the body of the old man in the way of the traffic to cause a disturbance and stop the procession had worked. He turned to face the other side of the archway.

Below him was the burlesque float.

Below him was Pippa.

She was in costume but he still recognised her from their brief encounter and the photographs he'd found in her house. Revenge keeps the senses keen. This was his chance, the police were at the other side of the old gates and it would take them a while to get back round. Whilst the distraction was in full flow it was time to act.

Punch leapt from the top of the archway and landed on the float covered in pink feathers and disco lights. Wildly he swung his bat at the performers. It caught one on her side and knocked her to the floor. The ragged nails tore a huge gash through her skin and blood gushed from the wound. The others screamed and hysterically ran in all directions, not knowing where to go but knowing they had to flee. Punch swiped his bat left and right, not aiming for anyone in particular but catching targets in the melee, the screams of his victims egging on his psychotic aggression. Pippa looked on, frozen with terror as she watched Punch get ever closer.

It took a good five minutes to battle through the panic-stricken crowd and fight the tide of terrified townsfolk as they fled the scene of the attack. By the time the police officers had reached the other side of the archway and boarded Pippa's float they found a scene worse than any they had yet encountered tonight. Girls lay in blood soaked pools, some dead already, others slowly fading from this life. Sally looked up at the officers with her one remaining eye; her left leg was split open at the thigh with a cut so deep you could see the splintered bone. Her jaw hung by slivers of muscle and was cracked in two whilst the right side of her face looked like it had been clawed off by some wild animal.

Sergeant Jack boarded the float and surveyed the chaos.

'Get an ambulance down here right now!' he barked at his dumbfounded team. 'Back those people up,' he gestured at the horrified crowd, 'nobody goes anywhere.'

He forced himself to look past the horrendous scenes of brutality and suffering that lay before him; he needed to check the float. Where was that murderous bastard Punch? And was Pippa among the wounded and dead?

'Damn it,' his heart sank as he realised, 'they've gone.'

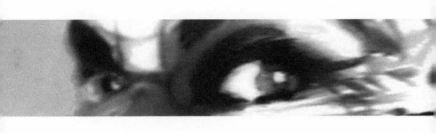

20

Pippa slowly came back to consciousness, her eyes drifting round the room as her brain made sense of her surroundings. The only source of light came from an ineffectual bulb that hung from the centre of the small room. It flickered and buzzed but seemed to leave more shadows than light in the darkened enclosure. There were no windows and only one door that she could make out; its rusty hinges staining the panels. The floors, walls and ceiling were all made of the same wood paneling that had blackened in the corners from damp and cultivated stretches of moss across its surface. The floor under her feet felt slippery and the air smelt musty and moist. As she regained control of her thoughts and body she found herself slumped on a small, wooden chair that creaked even under her sleight frame.

It was the next sight that caused her senses to sharpen. She tried to back away, tipping the chair up on its hind legs and sending both her and the rickety piece of furniture crashing to the ground. In front of her, just before the door, stood a small striped tent. She recognised it from her childhood as the Punch & Judy tent they used to watch on the beach. But this tattered, grimy canopy did not bring back any halcyon memories. The material was stained and mould grew on its surface creating foul patches of black. The edges were ragged and there were holes dotted throughout the covering, no doubt from the rats and mice that had chewed the fabric throughout its years of neglect.

It stood empty and still, but its eerie presence put Pippa into a panic. She quickly got to her feet and ran to the furthest corner away from the tent, pushing her body firmly against the opposite wall. She grabbed the chair and held it in front of her like a weapon.

She paused for a moment, watching the tent, studying it for any movement, but nothing happened. Pippa knew she had to escape but the only door was on the other side of the small, dark room, behind the ominous object. Putting the chair down and not daring to breathe, the scared girl tip toed across the room, keeping her back to the wall at all times. Time slowed and her heartbeat raced as she approached the Punch & Judy tent. Step by step she made her way round the side and slowly to the door. Pippa wrenched the door handle, but it would not budge. She shook it in its frame and pushed and pulled, but despite its decrepit appearance the door stood strong and blocked her exit.

Turning back to the tent for fear that her sudden noise might have awoken something unpleasant she was just as unsettled to discover it remained still. Its monolithic lack of motion taking on a menacing power of its own.

As slowly as she had crept round it to the door, Pippa crept back, all the while her gaze was fixed on the battered, old tent. A whisper began to swirl around the room, so faint to begin with that she couldn't pinpoint exactly when it first caught her ears. But gradually the whisper increased in volume.

What was it saying? Where was it coming from?

It could be coming from the tent but Pippa couldn't be sure. Her curiosity grew and she found herself edging towards it. The front had a large square opening where the performance would usually be played out, but this remained empty and in shadow. Slowly she inched her head closer and closer. What was that sound? Could she see something in there? If she could get just get that little bit closer…

She screamed in fright and fell backwards as the puppet of Mr Punch burst into the performance window of the booth, laughing in his characteristically crazed manner. Pippa tried to catch her balance but failed and fell back into the chair she had woken on. It creaked under the impact of her landing.

With nowhere to run and no way to fight she stared, transfixed on the bizarre sight in front of her.

'Hello Pippa,' the puppet Mr Punch began, 'what a lovely day. It is nice to be by the sea.'

The puppet's arms flailed around with the wild exaggerated movements he made.

A female puppet appeared, but not that of Judy.

'Helllllloooo,' Mr Punch whooped, 'who is this pretty lady?'

'Hello Mr Punch,' the female puppet replied,

'my name is Polly.'

'Pretty Polly I should say. You are beautiful,' he swooned, 'would you like to have dinner with me?'

'Oh Mr Punch,' the high pitched voice of Polly shrieked, 'you are very handsome. I would dearly love to do that.'

'I'll go get ready,' said Mr Punch.

He disappeared from view and was replaced by the puppet of a boxer, with long extending arms.

'You don't want to go anywhere near him Pretty Polly,' the boxer spoke in a low gruff voice, 'Mr Punch is a bad man.'

The boxer placed his mouth to Polly's ear and mimed a whisper to her.

'Oh no!' Polly cried.

With that the boxer ducked from view and Mr Punch re-entered.

'I'm ready Pretty Polly,' Mr Punch called excitedly, 'let's go.'

'Oh Mr Punch! I've heard all about you and what you did. How could you! I never want to see you again.'

Disgusted by the stories she'd been told Polly left the performance. The boxer reappeared laughing with a broad tone as he emerged in view.

'Take that Mr Punch,' he scoffed as his long arms hit the other puppet in the face. 'We don't want you here, no-one does.'

Mr Punch hollered in slapstick pain. The boxer ducked from view and was replaced by a police constable.

'Alright Mr Punch, we've heard you've been

causing trouble' the policeman said knowingly.

'No, no, no. It wasn't me. I haven't done anything,' Mr Punch protested.

'We've heard that all before, believe me.' The constable waved his arm to suggest a wagging finger, 'You're going to prison.'

'Noooooo!' Mr Punch wailed as both puppets exited.

For a moment there was silence. Pippa was mesmerized, still in shock from the events of the evening and unable to fathom what was happening next.

A backdrop appeared in the booth's performance. It was grey and had pictures of bars like a jail. Mr Punch appeared, his head hung low.

'Oooooh no. I'm in prison, what is to become of me?'

A hangman appeared with his black hood. Mr Punch stopped sobbing and took notice of the entrant.

'Not the noose,' Mr Punch cried. 'Please hangman, I don't deserve the noose!'

The hangman replied very solemnly, 'I've come to inform you, Mr Punch, that your house has been burnt down. Everything you owned and cherished has been destroyed. You have nothing. You are nothing. You may as well have the noose.'

With his grave news delivered the hangman left Mr Punch.

The poor puppet sobbed as he considered his predicament, 'What am I to do? I have nothing left, nothing!'

As Mr Punch sat in his cell and drowned in despair a puppet of the Devil suddenly appeared.

'Hello Mr Punch,' the Devil spoke in a cool and collected manner.

'Oh no!' Mr Punch screamed with fear.

But the Devil was not there to harm Mr Punch, at least not in a way we might expect.

'Can you really let them get away with all this? Can you?' the Devil began. 'You have been beaten, humiliated and crushed when you have done nothing wrong. You have been punished when you are wholly innocent.'

'They have broken me,' he answered, 'what is there left for me in this world?'

The Devil's tone became more animated, 'Are you really going to let them get away with that? Are you?! They have taken your love, your life, your pride and dignity.'

'But what can I do?' Mr Punch asked.

'Make them pay, Mr Punch,' the Devil encouraged. 'I have opened the cell door for you. And don't forget this,' the head of hell picked up Mr Punch's bat and handed it to its rightful owner. 'Make them pay.'

'Martin!'

Grete called out as she walked to the pier, her voice swallowed up by the wind that gusted down the beach. She held on to Kaspar's hand tightly as they made their way to the prearranged meeting place. The rain had got heavier since the sprinkling at the start of the carnival and Grete shielded her hand in front of her face to keep it dry from the spray. Had the weather not begun to turn so bad then maybe the crime scene tape would have still been fixed into position, instead of crumpled on the floor lying in a puddle of seawater and sand. The mother and son walked over the trashed and muddied tape without realising it was even there.

Pippa's private show continued. The prison backdrop had gone and in view were the puppets of Mr Punch and the boxer.

'Hello Mr Boxer,' Mr Punch called out, 'hit me will you? Punish me for a crime I am innocent for? I'm going to make you pay. Yes that's right.'

The puppet took his wooden stick and hit the boxer, thwak after thwak, until he lay down dead. The puppet hung over the side of the tent, his long arms hanging past his head.

No sooner had the boxer been disposed of than a crocodile appeared eating a string of sausages. Its jaws snapped as they opened and closed.

Mr Punch eyed the reptile, 'Oh no! You mean to punish me too? You won't get in the way of my revenge! Take that!'

With mighty swings of his bat the crocodile didn't stand a chance. He dropped his sausages and hung over the edge of the tent next to the boxer.

A clown puppet appeared and observed the carnage.

'Oh Mr Punch, what have you done?' the clown was given a high-pitched voice much like that of Pretty Polly.

'Hello Jo,' Mr Punch spoke to the puppet, his voice beginning to quiver from a simmering rage of insanity, 'you're going to get it too!'

'But I haven't done anything. It wasn't me.'

The voice of the clown was spoken in singsong manner as the puppeteer mocked her words.

'It wasn't you,' the contempt spat from his voice, 'it wasn't me. It wasn't any of us was it? Take that,' he swung his bat, hitting the clown, 'and that and that. That's the way to do it.'

Mr Punch beat the clown a few more times. Instead of draping the play dead puppet over the side of the tent like the others the puppeteer seemed caught up in his anger and threw it wildly across the room.

'Jo!' Pippa mouthed as she began to understand the significance of the last scene.

'All these lovely dead bodies.' Mr Punch surveyed his puppet massacre, 'Revenge is so much fun! But I must find the one that caused all this mess. Who spread the lies in the first place? Ah yes, Pippa, that evil little girl.'

Kaspar and Grete took shelter from the rain by the dodgems stand. The pier was empty and all the lights were off. Grete began to doubt the arrangement. Perhaps Martin had found better things to do than put on a private puppet show tonight.

'Martin?' Grete called out into the storm.

'Where is he Mum?' Kaspar asked as his patience began to wear.

'I don't know,' she replied.

As they waited in the rain Kaspar noticed something across the pier. It was hard to make out due to the flock of seagulls that had surrounded it. The young boy moved closer to get a better look.

'Have you seen Pippa?'

The show had become increasing sinister as the Mr Punch puppet asked a puppet of a plate spinner for the whereabouts of the girl.

When he failed to answer, the hook nosed anti-hero bashed him with his stick until the plate spinner's neck broke and he was thrown to the floor.

'There you are Pippa,' Mr Punch said as a detailed puppet of girl dressed in a black and pink basque appeared.

Pippa looked at herself sat in the chair wearing the same costume.

'Get away from me Mr Punch!' the Pippa puppet cried.

'I'm going to get you,' Mr Punch warned.

'Kaspar, come away from there,' Grete scolded her child.

'What is it Mum?' the boy asked, ignoring her telling off.

As he got closer to the flock he could begin to make out the object. It seemed to be roughly the size of a football, but much more solid. And what was that smell?

Intrigued he shooed the gulls away.

'Now I have you!' the Mr Punch puppet had found his finale in tonight's performance and caught the Pippa puppet. 'You have been a naughty girl haven't you? Telling lies about Mr Punch.'

'Please Mr Punch,' pleaded the Pippa doll, 'I am

so sorry. I didn't mean to-'

'You had ten years,' Mr Punch screeched in a furious frenzy, 'ten years to tell the truth. I rotted in prison all that time. Did you know the other prisoners found out what I was convicted for? And once they'd found out I didn't stand a chance. They beat me. They raped me. They broke me!'

Pippa subconsciously shook her head and a tear ran down her cheek.

Mr Punch continued, 'Can you imagine what that was like for me? Can you even begin to comprehend the complete humiliation I suffered every night? I can't close my eyes without fear of being attacked. My dreams are plagued. You could have freed me at any time. YOU could have stopped my torment.'

The Pippa puppet answered back with a mocking whine, 'I didn't want to Mr Punch because I'm a vile, stuck up little bitch! I'm nothing more than a whore that deserves everything I get. I walk around town like I own the place. I had everything when I was a child but still I had to steal money from you. And when I was caught red handed I couldn't just accept responsibility, no, instead I had to shoot my stupid mouth off. I had to fill the town's ears with evil words. Tell them you made me touch you. Tell them you told me not to tell. Tell them you made me promise. Tell them you were a dirty pervert.'

'And for that you must suffer!' screamed Mr Punch as the puppet beat the Pippa doll with his bat. The beating became more violent and exaggerated as he screamed each insult, 'You must suffer and die! Bleed and break! Bitch! Die! Die! Fucking, Pippa, die! That's the way to do it!'

The puppeteer threw the doll across the room in fit of rage.

Mr Punch's voice suddenly became eerily calm, 'That was fun, but it's no substitute for the thrill of real life. Where is the real Pippa?'

The puppet scanned around the room before fixing his sight on the girl sat in the chair, his beady eyes aimed straight into hers.

'Oh yes,' he began with a smug tone that raised to a crazed call, 'there she is!'

The Punch and Judy tent was torn to shreds as Punch exploded from it and swung his bat, the nails shredding the fabric as he made his dramatic entrance. He lunged at Pippa but she dodged, the chair that had been beneath her smashed into pieces as the bat crashed down. She tried the door again but it still wouldn't budge. With cat like reflexes she jumped against the wall, narrowly missing another swipe of Punch's weapon. It caught the door handle, breaking the knob clean off and destroying the lock. His next swing was not so lucky for Pippa as it managed to catch her. The nails pierced her calf muscle, tearing chunks of flesh from her leg. She screamed in pain, only metres from the exit.

Blood pumped from her wound as she held her injury. Unable to escape from the murderous lunatic all she could do was watch as he raised the bat above his head, ready for the deathblow.

The gulls were not giving up their secret easily, but with a little bit of bravery and a little bit of persistence Kaspar scared them away. Although he might have wished he hadn't. As the birds flew away they revealed the crushed and broken head of a woman. Her eyes and nose had been devoured by the hungry birds and they had pecked through the torn neck wound, pulling brain matter across the wooden decking.

The woman's feathered earrings shimmered in the wind.

It was the head of Polly!

Grete screamed in horror.

Her scream was so loud it startled Punch. Pippa used this momentary sliver of confusion and dived towards the door. Punch swung but missed. His bat hit the ground with a huge thump, driving the nails deep into the wooden floor. Wrestling with his weapon he pulled and twisted, trying to free it from where it had stuck fast.

Pippa opened the door and found herself on the pier. She had been in one of the storage huts all this time! She tried to run, but the pain from her leg was too great. Falling to the floor in tears she called for help. The police were stretched with sorting out the mayhem at the carnival. Pippa soon realised she would not find a saviour here.

'You can't run from me you naughty little girl!' Punch screamed as he freed his bat.

Getting back to her feet Pippa's legs began to wobble, unable to support her weight for any length of time. It was no use running, he'd be on her in an instant. Hearing his footsteps getting closer she knew her only chance was to hide.

Half running, half crawling she forced herself through the pain and got to the nearest attraction. She dived inside and hoped to hide.

The entrance was painted in faded red and yellow stripes and framed in a row of red light bulbs that flashed in a random sequence, revealing a number of them to no longer be working. Above the doorway a sign proclaimed in letters that ended in tails like lightning bolts: *The World Famous Maze Of Mirrors*.

21

Pippa stumbled into the maze with its labyrinth of reflective walls and dead ends. Immediately she fell into a mirrored wall and banged her head. She held her hands out and hobbled round the corridors unsure of where she was going. The more lost she could get the better chance she had of hiding. It wouldn't take long for Punch to track her down, the wound from her leg left a gory trail of blood like a scene from a nightmarish Hansel and Gretel. The pain seared up her leg with each step but she gritted her teeth and willed herself forward.

'You can't hide from me forever,' the voice of Punch echoed round the maze, 'this is my domain, little girl.'

Suddenly Pippa saw the reflection of Punch bounce off the mirrors, causing a vision of multiple maniacs as each reflection produced another on its adjacent wall. She jumped with fright. The images disappeared as suddenly as they came. Pippa turned in all directions. Where was he?

Quick glimpses of the crazed killer appeared and disappeared again as he strode through the attraction casting reflections all around her.

'There is no escape from me,' he taunted.

Pippa fell to the floor; the agony of her leg was proving too much. As she crawled along the floor his reflections appeared again, the evil, twisted face reproduced countless times.

'I'm going to enjoy killing you the most,' came his sinister threat.

The terrified girl crawled into a corner pushing her back against the wall. She couldn't stand the pain any longer and hope deserted her. Pippa buried her head into her knees to hide the sobbing and prayed that when he found her the end would be quick.

As she awaited death a voice floated down the twists and turns of the maze.

'The trail goes off in here.'

'Pippa? Miss Starr?' another voice called out. 'Are you there?'

PCs Knew and Rawlings had made their way back to the pier in a search of Pippa. Cautiously they made their way into the Maze of Mirrors calling out for the missing girl.

'Are you looking for me?' Punch responded as countless images of him walking by filled their view for a second.

'We're armed,' Rawlings shouted back, hoping to call his bluff. He took hold of his canister of PAVA ready to spray it, should they get close enough.

'But where am I?' Punch taunted. 'Am I here?'

Punch appeared down the end of a corridor.

The two officers ran down the end and sprayed the canister, only for it to squirt onto a mirrored wall. It was just a reflection!

'Or here?' Punch sneered.

PC Knew turned to see Punch next to him. He squeezed on his PAVA nozzle but again it just hit a mirror.

'I could be anywhere.'

With that the corridor erupted with images of the most wanted man in Stanswick Sands. Every wall looked like an exit, and in front of every exit stood the evil Punch. Knew and Rawlings turned in circles, looking at each image in a state of frightened bewilderment.

Hearing the two officers Pippa had regained her courage and staggered round the corner, trying to find her would be saviours. The moment she clocked them she called out.

'He's behind you!'

Punch swung his weapon to reveal he had been stood next to PC Knew. Knew was hit in the stomach and thrown against the wall opposite, shattering the mirror. The nails in the bat tore open his belly and as Knew fell to his knees he watched his own intestines spill from the wound, landing in a gory mess by his feet. He looked to PC Rawlings with an expression of sadness as he toppled forwards, collapsing face first on the floor.

Rawlings spun round looking for Punch, but again was confronted by a host of images. Most were reflections, but which one was real?

In anger and hatred he threw his canister at one of them. It struck the mirror cracking it in several places, distorting the reflection and making the image of Punch look even more twisted and malformed. Punch laughed manically at the policeman's frustration.

Revealing his hiding place to be in plain sight next to Rawlings, Punch swung his bat. He hit the officer square on the head, crushing his skull and piercing his brain. PC Rawlings was dead before he hit the ground.

Punch turned to Pippa who cowered in the corner.

'No more messing around,' he bellowed, 'I've had enough of your time wasting!'

His crazed insanity bore an even deadlier edge of frustration as he marched towards his prey. He swung his bat left then right as he made his way down the corridor, smashing each mirrored wall as he went. Reflective fragments rained from the cracked mirrors like a downpour of stars, whilst fury ignited the air. Lost in the maze, Pippa had nowhere left to run. At last he would have his blood soaked revenge.

22

Pippa closed her eyes and covered her face with her arm for protection. Even the police couldn't save her, what chance did she stand alone? Punch's vile bloodlust had seen no bounds on his quest for vengeance and she was the main prize. A prize that had been cornered and lay only a few feet from his grasp.

Seemingly from out of nowhere a small hand tugged at Pippa's wrist.

She opened her eyes to see a small boy looking up at her.

'Follow me,' Kaspar said.

Grasping her hand Kaspar led the limping girl through the maze with expert precision. His playtime on the pier was put to good effect as he guided her through the twisting corridors and fake exits. Looking back Pippa saw Punch give chase, his destructive onslaught continuing as he destroyed each mirror he passed.

'Come on,' Kaspar pleaded, pulling at her arm, 'hurry up.'

It wasn't long before the small boy's navigation took them through the exit and back outside, onto the pier. But the murderous peril was right behind them and gave chase until eventually they found themselves backed against the railings with nowhere left to run. The only path off the pier was being blocked by the devious Punch.

Kaspar took to his heels and ran headlong at their pursuer. Pippa screamed for him to come back but the boy did not care for her concern. Such big bravery from the young child was not rewarded however as Punch swung his fist at Kaspar and swatted him to the floor. The strike had connected hard and knocked the boy unconscious. Punch walked over to where he lay and raised his bat above his head, ready to deliver a mortal blow to the helpless child.

'You've been a naughty boy haven't you? Time to be taught some manners,' he shrieked.

'Over here!' shouted Pippa waving her arms. 'It's me you want. I told all the lies. I destroyed your life.'

The distraction worked as Punch left the child and headed towards the wounded girl.

Pippa could still only hobble, but there was no way she was going to let that evil bastard kill the young boy. Her escape route back to dry land was still blocked but desperate to get away she made the painful dash a few metres to the big wheel and began to climb its structure.

The metal framework was wet and slippery. It was cold to touch and gradually turned her hands numb making it much more difficult to grip, but still she climbed. Fearing to look down in case the height made her dizzy she trained her eyes upwards. The wheel rattled as she felt Punch put his feet on the support beams and begin his chase up the attraction.

Punch pulled himself up and made short work of the distance between them. Within a few moments he was only metres away and by the time they'd climbed three quarters height of the wheel he was able to reach out and grab her foot. Pippa's hands slipped as he pulled her back. She fell a few inches before clasping hold of another beam, her hands stung with the impact. She kicked wildly and screamed hoping to draw attention from anyone that might be passing by. Her thrashing legs shook Punch's hold of her foot and knocked him off balance. He fell a few feet but caught himself and continued to climb back after her.

Pippa looked down at the dizzying height they had achieved and watched Punch crawl up the big wheel towards her. He made another grab but she scurried up the wheel a little more, putting her feet out of reach. Punch clumsily swung his bat, however his action and aim were hampered as he tried to hold on in the wind that blew about them. Throwing her legs to one side Pippa dodged the strike. The bat hit the framework hard and vibrations shook through his weapon causing him to lose grip of it through his gloves.

They both watched, entranced, as the bat plummeted to the ground.

Kaspar regained consciousness in time to watch Punch's bat hurtle towards him. It spun in the air as the blood soaked nails glinted in the moonlight, the sharp ends on course for his head. The boy closed his eyes tight as fear glued him to the floor.

Thud!

He opened his eyes to see the bat beside him, stood upright, the nails embedded into the decking of the pier only centimetres from his head. He turned to face away from his would be death and saw his mother running towards him. Grete looked at once concerned and relieved. She picked the boy up and cradled him in her arms.

Punch turned back to Pippa and continued his climb. He launched a hand at her foot again, grazing her ankle but just failing to get a fixed hold.

Shots fired out and the metal supports sparked between the hunter and hunted as bullets ricocheted off the wheel. Startled, Punch turned back to see four armed police kneeling on the ground with their rifles aimed at him. Beside them stood Sergeant Jack, his coat blowing in the wind.

'Careful,' the sergeant shouted, 'you'll hit the girl. No firing until she is completely out the picture.'

The armed officers looked through their sights and watched as Pippa climbed out along the wheel and onto the roof of one of the ride's carriages.

Pippa stood on the roof of the carriage right near the top of the ride. It wobbled slightly in the wind and rain but she was able to keep her balance despite the weather conditions that made the daring escape even more hazardous.

She watched Punch crawl across the structure

and slowly plant his feet on the roof, searching for assurance of grip. It was too high to jump and there was no path back onto the wheel, her only option was the carriage she stood on. Braving the risk of falling, Pippa crouched by the edge, swinging her legs out and lowering herself down. Carefully she began to guide herself into the safety of the carriage. As her feet landed on the solid metal flooring she felt a sense of relief, but that was only fleeting as Punch's hand reached round from the roof and caught her arm. She screamed in fright and tried to claw it off her, but his grip was vice like and resisted all attempts of escape. With surprising strength he began to pull her towards him.

'We can't make the shot,' one of the gunman complained. 'The wind is too strong and they're too close together. If we fire we might hit her.'

They watched from below, helpless, as Punch leant over the edge of the carriage and took hold of Pippa. He seemed to be trying to pull her out of the carriage window.

Sergeant Jack looked on in anger. There had been too many dead at the hands of this crazed psychopath, there had to be something they could do to save that poor girl.

'We've got to separate them somehow,' the gunman continued, shouting through the wind. 'We've got to get her clear.'

The hapless audience could only watch as Punch pulled Pippa half out of the carriage. Her screams battled through the wind and met their ears in short bursts of stifled terror as Punch got back to his feet in order to pull the girl clear of the car and back onto the roof.

Knowing the girl would be dead in a matter of minutes if they didn't do something Sergeant Jack ran to the bottom of the big wheel. He looked around at the controls and pulled a large lever. The engines started up and the attraction burst into life. Bright lights that ran up and down the ride flashed all colours of nauseating neon whilst queasy fairground music blurted its distorted pitch through funneled speakers and the wheel began its rotation.

The sudden flashes of light and noise startled Punch. He released Pippa and stumbled forwards. The momentum of the ride caused him to lose balance and he fell off the side. Pippa slid back into the carriage and onto the safety of the metal flooring, she turned to see Punch hanging on to the side by his fingertips. The carriage slowly continued its revolution and hung out over the pier, dangling Punch above the roaring, black sea.

His gloves began to slip on the wet, metal railing.

'Don't you think you've won,' he spat his curse at her. 'You gave me ten years of suffering and pain. I'll give you the same and more. You will never sleep safely again.'

As he delivered his empty promise his grip began to weaken. Little by little he lost his hold until his fingers slipped from his gloves.

Cursing as he fell he never took his eyes off Pippa until he landed into the cold, wet blackness; the water slowly enveloped him as if removing his entire existence. Piece by piece he disappeared into the nighttime ocean until the last visible remnant was a fixed, unflinching grin. It appeared to float on the surface for a while before being rubbed out by the crashing coastal tides.

J. R. Park

23

J. R. Park

Wet, bruised and bloody, Martin Powell sat cuffed in the back of a police car. His mask had been confiscated for evidence so what remained was a sorrowful sight to behold. His grey, ashen face poking out of the bright, colourful costume made him look more like a dismal clown than a cold hearted killer. He looked towards the ground with sad eyes and rocked slightly in his seat.

Sergeant Jack and PC Andrews drove him back to the station whilst the rain lashed down against the windscreen. As Martin spoke with a faint smile across his face the two could sense a defeated, almost peaceful weariness about him.

'Such a nice place,' he muttered, 'it was lovely to come back. So many things had stayed the same, but so many things have changed. Pippa had grown hadn't she?'

Jack leant backwards, tilting his ear towards the wretched man to make out what he was saying.

Martin continued, 'She was on my mind a lot

when I was inside. Didn't expect her to look so grown up when I came out. Silly really. She was on my mind a lot.'

PC Comer straightened the towel draped over Pippa's shoulders as they walked down the pathway to the young girl's family home. As they stepped through the front door Pippa saw the house in ruin. Everything had been turned upside down and smashed to pieces as if a tornado had blitzed a destructive course through the house. A few police officers had arrived just before them and were taking photographs of the recently discovered carnage in Quick Lane.

'I was at her house earlier today you know,' Martin continued to babble, 'now that hadn't changed much. She wasn't there when I called, but somebody was.'

His mind drifted back to earlier in the evening. He had burst into her house hunting for Pippa but found someone else instead. Punch had beaten the girl but she had escaped when the answer machine distracted him. He had toyed with some nails that had scattered across the floor whilst he listened to Pippa's message that came through on loud speaker:

Hi it's Pippa. Hope you're okay, the carnival is going great. The burlesque idea was brilliant. The judges seem to be really going for it and we are set to win. The procession is about to head off round the streets so I have to go. It's raining here but I'll be okay. So how's the baby doing? I hope Danny isn't too grizzly. He's been teething recently. Call me if you have any problems. Bye.

Shocked at the sight of devastation, Pippa began to shake her head in disbelief. PC Comer tried to hold her close, but the comforting officer was pushed aside as the nineteen year old rushed upstairs. All sense of pain disappeared from her wounds as her mind raced with thoughts of the worst possibilities. There were more officers upstairs, and as they turned to see Pippa running past them their faces contorted with horror.

The faint smile on Martin's face began to grow.

'She'll never forget old Mr Punch,' he said half laughing.

The officers tried to stop her but the more they tried the more her determination grew. Eventually she fought them off and ran into a small room beside the bathroom. The wallpaper was bright yellow with large murals of cartoon animals decorated around the middle.

'Smack the baby.'

Bloodstains were sprayed across the child-like menagerie in contrast to the innocent smiles of the painted characters. In the centre of the room, suspended from the ceiling, fragments of a mobile spun in small circles.

'Smack the baby.'

Broken shards of a wooden cot lay in a crumpled pile underneath the mobile remains, entwined with strewn bedding and blankets stained red.

'Smack the baby.'

Pippa collapsed, overcome with grief.

Amongst the wreckage of splintered wood and blood soaked linen she caught sight of that she feared most. A sight no mother should see. Twisted and tangled in the timber and bedding lay the crushed and mangled corpse of her lifeless son.

'Smack the baby.'

ABOUT THE AUTHOR

J. R. Park lives on the edge of Bristol, England in a
shared house of seven. He is not married, has no
children and no pets. In fact he often wonders what he
has spent his adult life doing!
He started writing in 2013 after a long hiatus. Initially he
wrote poetry, but soon gravitated a year later to his genre
of choice after discovering the lurid delights found in the
works of author Guy N Smith.
He has hyper extendable joints and a wish to visit
Iceland one day.

TERROR BYTE – J. R. PARK

Street tough Detective Norton is a broken man.

Still grieving the murder of his girlfriend he is called to investigate the daylight slaughter of an entire office amid rumours of a mysterious and lethal computer program. As the conspiracy unfolds the technological killer has a new target.
Fighting for survival Norton must also battle his inner demons, the wrath of MI5 and a beautiful but deadly mercenary only known as Orchid.

Unseen, undetectable and unstoppable.
In the age of technology the most deadly weapon is a few lines of code.

TERROR BYTE

J.R. PARK

"Truly a horror tale for the modern digital age."
Duncan P Bradshaw, author of Class Three.

"Fast paced, action-packed, intricately plotted and filled
with technological paranoia."
Duncan Ralston, author of Gristle & Bone

"He manages to combine gore, sex, humour and
suspense with a gripping story line."
Love Horror Books

"J. R. Park's new novella Terror Byte could be the story
to bring horror back to technology based adventures."
UK Horror Scene

"Jesus. What the fuck is this?"
Vincent Hunt, creator of The Red Mask From Mars

UPON WAKING – J. R. PARK

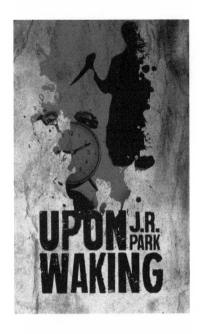

What woke you from your sleep?
Was it the light coming through the curtains? The traffic
from the street outside?

Or was it the scratching through the walls? The cries of
tormented anguish from behind locked doors? The
desperate clawing at the woodwork from a soul hell bent
on escape?

Welcome to a place where the lucky ones die quickly.

Upon waking, the nightmare truly begins.

UPON WAKING – J. R. PARK

"It's basically like John Doe's murderous fantasies in Se7en with Clive Barker dancing naked on top of it."
Daniel Marc Chant, author of Maldicion & Burning House

"Sick. Demands a re-read."
Duncan P. Bradshaw, author of Class Three

"Such vivid images. J. R. Park is a sick man." – Mistress Fi, fetish model

THE EXCHANGE – J. R. PARK

Unemployed and out of ideas, Jake and his friends
head into town for something to do.

But before long they are in over their heads.
Determined to get their friend back from the
clutches of a lethal and shadowy group, the teenagers
find themselves in possession of an object with
mysterious powers.

With their sanity crumbling amidst a warping reality,
the gang are cornered on a wasteland in the middle of
the city, caught in a bloodthirsty battle between criminal
underlords, religious sects and sadistic maniacs.

Nightmares become reality as the stakes begin to rise.
Who will have the upper hand and who will survive this
deadly encounter as they bargain for their lives in this
most deadly exchange.

Amazon reviewer comments:

"The most purely entertaining horror novel I've read this year. And it has unicorns!"

"The Exchange is the stuff of nightmares."

"A thrill ride of suspense, action and mystery."

"It is a real roller-coaster, packing in twists galore; plenty of gore, fascinating theologies and memorable protagonists."

For up to date information on the work of J. R. Park
visit:

JRPark.co.uk
Facebook.com/JRParkAuthor
Twitter @Mr_JRPark

For further information on the Sinister Horror
Company visit:

SinisterHorrorCompany.com
Facebook.com/sinisterhorrorcompany
Twitter @SinisterHC

Lightning Source UK Ltd.
Milton Keynes UK
UKHW040603241219
355963UK00001B/22/P